Dedication

To Mom and Dad

LanTell Publications

Author's Introduction

When I was five years old, my father told me the story of an agricultural laborer who broke his arm while harvesting grapes for a large manorial estate in Sicily. Wrapping the arm in a cloth sling, the unfortunate man threw it over his shoulder and kept picking.

"Why didn't he go home?" I asked my father, thinking of the times I was allowed to go home from school because I had a stomach ache or some other complaint. "He had to pick the grapes" was my father's reply. This puzzled my innocent young mind. Still more distressing to me was learning that the man's broken arm became infected soon after the harvest ended and that he died from the infection. The man in this tragedy was my great-grandfather.

I would say it is rare to be able to pinpoint the moment when a lesson or value becomes branded onto one's life view. Yet, this story of dedication and courage made and continues to make a remarkable impression on me.

There is no doubt that it would be years before I could accept that my great-grandfather needed to stay at his post to finish the essential business of bringing in the grapes. Over the years, the question of why he stayed became less critical in my eyes than that he did stay—whatever his motives—and that he paid the ultimate price for his fidelity. A faithfulness that raised him, in the hearts of his son, my grandfather, and his grandson, my father, to something of a family legend and icon.

My father told other stories about his family in Sicily and their varied fates in the New Worlds of North and South America. Like the tale of my great grandfather's death, most of these stories were somewhat perplexing to his children growing up in the 1960s and 1970s. Many of the actors in his narratives lived in a world where the singular objective was survival. A world of such stark simplicity that the ability to reach that goal was the only mark of success that mattered.

But if the concept and opportunity for what counts as a successful life today were absent from the lives of our not-too-distant ancestors, they had compensations that we can barely understand. Among them was the knowledge that people were far more important than the possessions that fill the relational vacuum of our lives today. The strong ties they had with friends, neighbors, and family were accentuated by the values that reflect and give my father's stories their compelling and inspiring quality. Values like hope, fidelity, loyalty, generosity, courage, and religious faith.

This, essentially, is why we listen to and cherish stories of people—and most especially family members—from the past. We want to know by what means they made what they could of what life had given them. How, every once in a while, they overcame their tribulations, turning the commonplace into a fable to inspire the generations who would live after them. It is my hope (and my father's, I venture to say) that his stories will likewise enlighten and inspire, but just as importantly, *entertain*, those who will read them.

Angela Edwards
November 14, 2019

Table of Contents

Author's Introduction 3

HARRY COHAN 7

ROSALIA'S REVENGE 39

VITA 51

PAOLO VISITS THE BARON 77

THE HAT 101

THE WITCH ON
BLEECKER STREET 127

Author's Notes 201

About the Author 207

Family Photos 209

HARRY COHAN

Harry Cohan was a big man. Six-foot-two and portly, his bulk rivaled that of the tenements on his lower West Side beat. Cohan seemed to wear the squalor that surrounded him. His coat drooped, and its brass buttons were smudged and dirty, much like the buildings of the precinct. Yet, he had a sure dignity, its epicenter in the New York City police badge on his chest. Cohan was the scourge of Thompson Street, and the local boys shouted "Aw, shit!" when they saw him coming. He could spot an open hydrant 30 yards away. He could hear a dice roll half a block away; and when he threw his nightstick, it flew with the velocity of Babe Ruth sliding into home plate.

He'd seen boys smarter than the ones in this neighborhood end up in the morgue, he would tell the gang. The gang being Louie D'addato and Frankie Castiglioni, Big Sal Pesce, Tappy Mannino, and Leonardo Caraciella.

"Did you play hooky last week?" Cohan would ask Leo.

"No, not me," the wiry ten-year-old answered, even if he had.

"Well, go to school. You got a good head on your shoulders. Put it to good use," Cohan would say, and drum his knuckles, not so softly, on Leo's head.

Leo loved to read, and he devoured anything he could find—Jack Armstrong paperbacks, magazines, municipal ordinances, the classics—in the alley below the fifth-floor apartment where he and his family lived. Immersed in a western, he'd hear Billy the Kidd gallop into the sunset, blink away the sun reflecting on gold battle standards while reading "Song of Roland." Then, out of nowhere, Cohan would appear.

"What're you reading, kid?" The policeman asked on the latest of these encounters.

"A book," Leo mumbled.

Cohan tilted the book with his nightstick to see the cover, while Leo stared at him nervously.

"Roland, eh? You were reading that last time I found you here. You like history, don't cha kid?"

Leo rolled his eyes, letting Cohan draw his own conclusions.

"I guess so..." the policeman mused. "You goin' to high school?"

The boy perked up immediately and nodded his head. "You better believe it," he told the policeman.

Most of the kids thereabouts left school early to earn money for their families. But not Leo. "I'm one of the few kids around here who *is* goin' to high school," he boasted. "I'm gonna build bridges, so maybe I'll go to Brooklyn Poly. But I can be anything I wanna be," he assured the policeman. "A chemist, or a pilot, or a Saracen!" And he swung his arm as if he was a Mohammedan brandishing a sword.

"My teacher says I'm good at public speakin'. You wanna hear the Gettysburg Address?!" He jumped on the curb and turned to face the policeman.

"NO!" Cohan shouted, stepping back. "I mean..." he squirmed, and Leo was reminded of a June bug he once saw trapped in a crack on the sidewalk. "Save that for your teacher."

Dejected, Leo stepped down to the street while the policeman glanced at his watch.

"Gotta go," said Cohan, whacking the boy on the back. "Curfew's ten." With that, he was gone, leaving Leo to rub his shoulder.

Leonardo closed his book and took a moment to listen to the surrounding city. The vendors' cries were fading, and the late afternoon rush hour was building to a roar of screeching automobiles and streetcars, whinnying horses, and loud pedestrians. Leonardo thought he heard his mother's voice, calling him in her Sicilian dialect. In any case, other mothers were hanging out of tenement windows to call *their* children. This was Leonardo's cue to return home, as well.

Turning onto Thompson, his shoulder aching, Leonardo felt a spark of anger at the way the policeman knocked or cudgeled him at every encounter. Yet, Cohan's words were encouraging, and in Leonardo's world, encouragement was not easy to come by.

Who would give it? Not the street vendors, selling wares from a sidewalk-fronted shop or an overloaded pushcart. They saw no need for an education. Nor would Leo's friends—Louie, Big Sal, Tappy, and Frankie. They were more interested in finding a stray, unlit cigarette in the gutter or an easily tapped candy stand. Or, for those with an extra nickel, a craps game behind a stable, where the game's excitement paralleled the risks of living on Thompson Street.

The horses, burdened with loads of milk and ice, couldn't acknowledge an "A" on an exam. Nor could the huge automobiles, their drivers sounding their horns with the sneer of modernity. The tired workmen, Leonardo's father among them, could mutter *e bene* on seeing a child's school report, yet wonder at the import of such an accomplishment. Sweat in a man's pores was what was needed to put food on the table for a family. Expecting better than this for one's children seemed as foolhardy as scaling the towers these workmen gambled their lives to raise.

Even at his tender age, Leo knew he wanted more than his immediate surroundings offered. He thought the same held true for many of his schoolmates and friends. Wasn't something they talked about, he just thought he knew. Build a bridge, travel the world, fly a biplane: these were the aspirations that badgered Leo day and night, and composed the foundation for his personality. While Leo and a select few of his schoolmates and friends had an abundance of such yearnings, he was nearly certain that his brother, Johnny, did not.

Like most of the kids thereabouts, Johnny Caraciella had left school at 14. Streetwise and cynical, the city energized him the way electricity lights a neon sign, giving him life and spirit that Leonardo envied. Johnny never looked farther than a corner game of craps for excitement, and the faces and colors of Thompson, Sullivan, Prince, Broome, and Spring Streets seemed enough of a world to satisfy him.

During the week he was learning to cut hair, shave beards, and give manicures at *Antonio D. Saluzio's* barbershop. But at night he ran errands for a local "entrepreneur." A man whose clothes and flash told Johnny he was a *somebody*, not one of the local nobodies whose lives broke their backs and spirits like victims of the evil eye in his parents' superstitions.

While Johnny's transgressions were adult, that didn't stop him from acting the child at times. Fresh out of school, he was in a limbo where games still appealed to him while adulthood beckoned. In typical fashion, Johnny found ways to accommodate both, and once he set his mind to it, had more ways to needle, skirt, poke, and provoke the law than a hardened criminal. That's why, when Johnny got it into his head to make trouble, Leo's heart pounded with hand-rubbing glee, even while his head urged him to run for home. At these times, Leo rarely listened to his head.

Johnny was ripe for one of these misadventures in late November of 1924. A Canadian Clipper froze the night air, and Harry Cohan's mood was foul. This became evident when he poked Big Sal with his nightstick, then soon afterwards chastised another kid for jaywalking, branding him an "Irish Mick".

"What's Cohan doin', callin' O'Neill a mick? Thought he was Irish himself," Tappy said.

"Nah, he ain't no pigshit," declared Louie. Thirteen and the oldest of Leo's friends, Louie saw himself as the boss of the group and an authority on all subjects. "That's Coh*e*n." Louie emphasized the *e*. "One of them goddamned Jew names."

Surrounded by so many nationalities—Irish uptown and west, Jews on Delancey Street, Russians, Poles, and Ukrainians on the East Side, Germans in the north of Manhattan—most of the gang could tell an Irishman from a Scot, an Italian from a Greek, a Hasidic Jew from an Orthodox Russian. Still, some names were stumpers. Unable to agree on the policeman's ethnicity, they dropped the subject to play marbles, producing some chalk to draw a circle on the crumbling sidewalk.

Leo threw himself into the game. He loved his friends. They flocked together on the streets because they needed allies to survive. Summer and winter, they were encouraged to stay outside—away from the contagions and stifling humanity of their tenement flats—by the same parents who said in America the children ran wild. Better, however, for them to live that way than to share the fate of scores of kids killed by tuberculosis—a malady that prowled the tenements like the cats at the Fulton Fish Market.

All the boys had an undeniable place in Leo's heart, but Frankie was far and above his favorite, though it was hard for Leo to say why exactly. Both were ten and lived in the same building; and they played Franks and Saracens together, something Leo couldn't get the other boys to do. But that wasn't all of it.

Leo finally decided he and Frankie were best friends because Frankie was so easy to get along with. Take, for instance, when Leonardo first started taking Rapid Advancement classes. He loved to tell the other kids what he was learning. But some of them didn't want to hear it.

These were tough guys. Guys like Red *LaRocca,* who was eventually expelled for hitting the principal, and Abe Feldsen, who charged kids a penny to cross the street where he lived. Guys like that didn't want to know about the Spanish-American War, and they beat you up if you tried to tell them something they didn't want to know.

So, Leo was knocked down on the playground a few times. In fact, it became a spectator sport, knocking Leo down. He could outtalk those guys. But he could never knock them down, the way they did him.

It happened twice one day. Blinded by rage, Leonardo bumped into Frankie as he climbed the stairs in his building. It just so happened that Frankie had a message from Leo's mother to put in an order for coal.

This made Leo furious. He knew they needed coal. And he didn't need Frankie telling him something he already knew.

"Shut up, Frankie!" Leo snapped.

Not comprehending Leo's mood, Frankie repeated himself: "Your mother needs coal, and ..."

Leo slugged Frankie before he finished. He didn't mean to. Really. His action was as much a surprise to Leo as it was to Frankie, and he was shocked by the "Smack!" when his fist hit Frankie's face. Nonetheless, Leo couldn't help but be delighted with the result: there lay Frankie, flat on the landing. One clip to the jaw put him there.

"I'm sorry, Frankie," Leo said, remorse filling him like water gushing from a hydrant, while he helped Frankie to his feet.

"It's okay." Frankie said, in a hurry to leave. "I'll order the coal."

Since that day, he and Frankie had been fast friends. Frankie hadn't taken it personally that Leo hit him. He understood that some guys had to let off steam. If anything, Frankie deferred to Leo more than he used to, and Leo was soon going out of his way for Frankie as well. One clip to the jaw, that's all it took for him to go down. Leo had to like a guy like that!

It wasn't so easy for Leo to like his brother Johnny. Whereas Frankie made him feel like a heavyweight contender, Johnny's effect on him was the opposite. Where Johnny excelled, Leo was an insignificant gnat. And where Leo excelled, Johnny ignored his efforts.

Here, for instance, was Johnny, walking up the street, headed for Leo and his friends. Johnny's head was in constant motion, nodding left and right to people he knew, whereas Leo walked that street like a hick just off the train from Poughkeepsie. But Johnny excited attention from everyone. The confident way he walked in time to the surrounding chaos drew glances from youths, like Leonardo, who envied his looks and street suave.

"Hey, Leo!" he said, as he came close.

Leo was surprised by his enthusiasm. They saw each other every morning and night. What was there to get excited about? Leo surmised then that his brother had gotten into another argument with their father. And he braced himself to see how this unpleasantness had affected Johnny.

"What's up, Johnny?" Louie asked. All Leonardo's friends were impressed by Johnny, but Louie worshipped him.

This annoyed Leonardo. What was so great about Johnny? He was good looking. So what? His friends were the carefree, lighthearted ones. So what, again? Leonardo had a hunch that most of them had a jail sentence in their futures.

"I just came by to see how you fellas are doin'," said Johnny.

More likely he was there to remove himself from their father's wrath, Leo ruminated.

"What're you playing?" Johnny asked, taking in the chalk circle and scattered marbles on the sidewalk.

"Aaaah—they wanted to play marbles." Louie gave Johnny a we-men-of-the-world-are-above-this look. "But I was really in the mood for some poker."

"Well, Louie," Johnny pulled out a cigarette as he spoke. "Poker's my game. Fact is..." he leaned towards Louie confidentially. "I got a pack of cards here I ain't even cut yet. You guys'll like this," he added, with a wink.

The boys rushed to look, crowding together like pigeons on the sidewalk. As usual, Johnny didn't disappoint them, for the back of the cards featured a woman voluptuously posed in the nude. Big Sal let out a long, low whistle, and Leonardo drew irresistibly closer despite himself. He and Frankie opened their eyes wide in disbelief, but they covered this up with their best stabs at nonchalance.

"Look at that!" Leo enthused.

"I'd like to get to know that baby!" Frankie said.

"Wait a few years and maybe you will. She puts on a show in Jersey City," Johnny informed Frankie. "She's a stripper."

"That right?" Louie quipped. "Well, maybe I can hitch a ride and say hello while she's leaving her dressing room. I'll bet I know how to treat a girl like that!"

Frankie snorted. "If she meets you in the alley she might get sick and faint." Leo laughed at Frankie's cleverness, followed by the rest of the boys.

"Don't pay no attention, Louie," Johnny tried to comfort the other boy. "They say she don't have nothin' to do with you if you ain't got money, anyway."

"How do you know so much about her, Johnny?" Tappy asked. "You been in the theater while she was strippin'?"

"Nah, I ain't of age, yet. I got some older friends. They told me about her." Johnny shrugged his shoulders as if these revelations were nothing.

"Was it Leadpipe or Cokey Joe that told you about her?" Leo asked, finally letting his jealousy get the better of him. He thought some of Johnny's glamour might rub off if he revealed that his brother knew some of the neighborhood's worst young criminals. Predictably, Johnny backed away from the question. "Of course not. I ain't seen them in ages, Leo. You know that."

Humph, Leonardo smirked. Not for the ages since last Saturday. But he decided not to bring that up. Instead, he joined his friends as they gathered to begin the card game.

"Hey, Leo," Johnny said, his voice resounding, as all of theirs did, with the brusque accent of the neighborhood. He kept up a perfect rhythm as he dealt. "It's cold out here," and he shot Leo a look that seemed to say the younger boy should do something about the temperature.

Leo shrugged. It was just like his brother to hold him responsible for the weather. "If you don't like it, move to Florida."

Johnny laughed. "He's a kidder," Johnny informed the other boys. "You oughtta hear him at home—too much. But seriously, I got an idea."

Leonardo cringed. Ideas from Johnny rarely took the form of a starburst. Usually, they were more like volcanoes.

"What?" Leo asked.

"Why don't we build a fire?"

So that was it. Building bonfires was a way the boys amused themselves and kept warm during cold evenings. But lately Cohan had been trying to discourage these fires because they damaged the road. Leonardo threw his cards down in panic.

"Cohan said no fires! They melt the asphalt and put holes in the pavement! He said the next guy who put a hole in this road was in trouble!"

"There are already so many holes in this road it looks like a piece of Swiss cheese," Johnny shot back. "One more ain't gonna make a difference."

Leo writhed with frustration. They'd end up making a bonfire, alright. Once his brother had a notion, it practically took a wrecking ball to knock it out of his head. As for Leo's friends, they were sold on the idea as soon as it came out of Johnny's mouth.

Even Frankie. "There's plenny a' wood in back of Rohman's," he told Johnny, excitedly.

"Good enough for a fire?" Johnny asked warmly.

"And how! We'll have a fire goin' til D'Costa comes troo wid da milk truck in the morning," Big Sal effervesced.

"Well, what do you boys say?" Johnny turned the matter over to Big Sal, Tappy, Louie, and Frankie. Their enthusiasm confirmed what Leo already knew—a sensible argument was nothing pitted against Johnny's charisma, and events unfolded as they always did. Though Leo always swore he'd never again follow one of Johnny's schemes, he invariably forgot his objections when in the spirit of making mischief with his buddies. For just as Big Sal, Louie, Tappy, and Frankie would jump into a bottomless manhole with Johnny, Leo would gladly follow his friends down Niagara Falls in a barrel.

They quit the card game, and each boy began to do his part to build the fire. Louie and Big Sal picked up the discarded wood from the back lot of Rohman's Furniture and Upholstery, Leo and Frankie gathered kindling, and Tappy and Johnny searched for a place where a small fire would attract the least attention and alarm.

They settled on a sliver of street at Sullivan and West 3rd, a corner with such an unsavory reputation, even Cohan patrolled the area infrequently. But the boys knew the real criminals would leave them alone, for what did they have that anybody wanted? As for the surrounding tenement dwellers, well, from behind their locked doors they'd think the *boys* were criminals and curse them for it, while refusing to call the police, whom they distrusted more.

As predicted, the wood burned crisply, warming the boys and buoying their spirits as they played penny ante poker. They caught and made a snack of the easy to catch sparrows that proliferated on the streets. Tappy told them ghost stories, and they let Leo tell them how he dissected a frog in biology class. But it was Johnny who dominated the evening, delighting them with stories of adventures that the others, mindful of Old-World parents, would be unlikely to join in. But their enjoyment was to be short lived.

Johnny was telling them how he and his friends had discovered a way to sneak onto a Coney Island roller coaster without paying when a window opened above their heads. The boys looked up to see a large figure silhouetting the light escaping the window.

"Eh!" this figure boomed. "*Non brusciati! Volete comminciare uno fuoco?!*"

There was a startled silence. This was not what Leo and his friends expected. Usually it was Cohan, not the tenants, who objected to the bonfires, and they made a brave attempt to ignore the man.

"Hey!" The man boomed louder. "*S'facimo*! Put that fire out!" He leaned over the windowsill to peer at their faces.

"Go suck a lemon!" Frankie answered, to the astonishment of Leo and his friends. Normally, Frankie would have retreated before the man's insults, but he was likely emboldened by Johnny's presence.

"Oh yeah?" The man replied. "Go suck your mother's tit! All of you!"

That did it. Johnny, Leo, Leo's friends, and the man began yelling an entire dictionary of maledictions at each other. After Frankie's preemptive strike, it was Johnny, naturally, who led the charge. He shouted louder than anyone, and when Leo and his friends became hoarse and worried by the curious heads popping out of windows to the left and right, Johnny and the man kept hollering.

Leo watched in admiration and dread. Johnny was a corker. He was also getting them into trouble. For just then, Leo saw Harry Cohan arrive on the scene. He was running towards them with nightstick in hand, shouting.

"YOU LITTLE BASTARDS! I TOLD YOU NO FIRES ON THE ASPHALT! I'LL TAKE THE WHOLE LOT OF YOU INTO THE STATION!! I'LL HAVE YOU IN PINSTRIPES UNTIL YOU'RE NINETY!!!"

The boys never saw Cohan so angry. He thundered towards them with steam billowing from his mouth, his chest heaving like a subway clamoring on the El. His eyes big and frightening, his face redder than a hook and ladder engine, it seemed he would explode if he didn't get to them first.

"Jesus Christ. The sonofabitch flipped his lid," Johnny marveled.

That worried Leo. When Johnny was scared, it was trouble.

The boys threw down their cards, then took off down the alley like rats. Instinctively, they ran to the back of the closest tenement, while the building's occupants gawked, and Cohan followed closely.

They scrambled along the back of the building, down the alley straddling its west side, then back on West 3rd Street, past where the fire burned unchecked. Ahead—obstructing their way across McDougal—stood a fruit cart, waiting to be put away for the night. The boys stopped.

"Jump over it!" Johnny ordered, coming up from behind.

One at a time they hopped, apples and squash rolling onto the street like pool balls over a billiards table. Once that obstacle was cleared, they encountered a horse standing in the street halfway down McDougal. Each of them ducked under it, convinced the policeman couldn't match their dexterity. But when they glanced back, Cohan was still only a stone's throw away. They redoubled their efforts, the rhythmic smacking of their feet like applause during amateur night in one of the nearby theaters.

They finally came to the end of McDougal, where they encountered the blocks of rubble left by the wrecking balls of the 6th Avenue expansion project. Making a quick right onto Spring Street, they ran straight towards the Irish section. Then, at the intersection of Spring and Varick Streets, they had a choice looming before them.

Leo considered their options in silence. They could go back into lower Manhattan's Italian section, scampering up alleys and ducking behind garbage cans, until they could slip home, undetected. Or they could go west, past Hudson Street, to hide in the Irish section. An only slightly less dangerous alternative to this would be to go past the Irish neighborhoods to the docks. Or, more accurately, to "the Farms"—a wide stretch of cobblestones offering sanctuary from both Cohan and vindictive Irish street gangs.

They slowed down as the bustling Irish business center on Varick Street became visible. Finally, Johnny signaled them to halt.

"The Farms," he said. There was no need to say more.

Later, Leo wondered how his friends could so trustingly follow anyone, even Johnny, into the "Farms" at night. To be sure, there was a good deal of muttering when Johnny was out of earshot.

Located on the island's west side, "the Farms" was a misnomer for an area that once was farmland, stretching south and west of the city limits, but had been transformed decades ago into a long, flat plain of cobblestones running along the Hudson River docks, flanked on the city side by railroad tracks used for cargo transport. During the day, the Farms was filled with commercial vehicles and longshoremen. At night, the area was mostly unlit and deserted, a perfect setting for stories of murder and mayhem. And enough bodies had been pulled from the river into the Farms for Leo and his friends to know these accounts were more than "just stories."

Besides braving the Farms at night, Leonardo and his friends would have to walk through the Irish neighborhoods to get there. The alternative to all this was certain incarceration. If it wasn't for Johnny, thought Leo, they'd all turn themselves in. But it was Johnny's way to climb the highest building when it was in his way, and the way of his young compatriots to follow, even if it meant dangling from his suspender straps to do so.

The passage through the neighborhoods west of Hudson was surprisingly uneventful. While the spectacle of a group of Italian boys stampeding up their boulevards and alleys alarmed the Irish residents, they were calmed to see a policeman chasing them. One or two even cheered him on: "Go get 'em, Cohan!"

(That settles it...Leonardo thought. That guy is *not* Jewish.)

The boys moved past Varick and down Hudson, using tactics that didn't exactly repel Cohan, but did keep him out of nightstick-striking distance. At the end of Hudson, they passed through Duane Park, and then, walking west on Chambers Street, they came to the dimly lit, lunar landscape of the Farms.

They looked over the plain in silence. Leo could tell his friends didn't want to go in there. Nonetheless, they were losing precious seconds by hesitating. It was Big Sal who broke the spell. "Let's cross the tracks here, where there's light," he suggested.

"Good thinkin'." Johnny commended him. Groping around in the dark as they were, it was too easy for one of them to fall over the railroad lines and break a leg. Blocks of warehouses stood on the city side of the tracks, some of them lit with spotlights. In one of these dim pools of light they crossed the tracks, placing themselves on the outer edge of the Farms.

Picturing the sweeping expanse of cobblestones seen in daylight, Frankie and Leo started to break into a run. Leo soon found himself on the ground, however, his shoulder and arm smarting from taking the brunt of his fall. A few feet away lay Frankie; close to him, Louie.

"It's ice!" Louie shrilled. "Goddamn it, we'll break our asses! I say we double back to Thompson." All heads turned to Johnny, as Leo and his friends reeled with pain.

"Yeah, we could do dat," Johnny agreed. He swung his head around to see if Cohan had set his sights on them yet. "But if we can break our asses, Cohan can break his, too."

"And ain't he got a big one!!" Big Sal smart-alecked.

"That's right," Johnny nodded. "The bigger they are, the harder they fall." He looked at Leo and Frankie. "You two—didja ever go sledding on ice?"

"Hell, we don't need a sled. We can just slide on dis stuff," Frankie answered. And then Frankie and Leo looked at each other, open-mouthed. Almost at once, each flung himself on the ice, first backing up a little, then diving. They ended up with chins tucked in and legs extended behind them, Peter Pan style. The ice, a smooth, glacial expanse, brought them midway between the beginning of the Farms and the docks.

"Cohan can't do dat," Johnny assured the other boys. Confident the matter was settled, he turned to Frankie and Leo and pointed to some loading machinery in the distance. "Meet us dere."

When Leo and Frankie reached their destination, they quickly ducked behind the base of a looming crane, its steel hook dangling. Leo peered between the grizzled treads of the crane and its muddied footrest, watching Johnny and the other boys dive onto the ice. In a few seconds they were gliding right up to the crane, with a few mishaps.

Louie, for one, crashed headfirst into the crane's mud-caked grill. (Leo and Frankie laughed soundlessly at this.) And Tappy almost landed in the river! It took all their might for Leo and Frankie to yank him back safely onto the dock again. Finally, the boys sat in a circle, the vapor from their exhalations forming one frosty cloud as they waited for Big Sal to join them.

In a moment, they heard Big Sal slide across the ice, ending close to where they were sitting. He gasped for air as he struggled to his knees. "Cohan saw me!" he spit out.

Johnny shrugged. "He ain't comin' here."

"Maybe not him, but he brought some people with him. A coupla' guys, and some kids wid a sled," Big Sal declared.

"Christ," Johnny muttered.

Leonardo swallowed a huge lump in his throat, while the other boys looked at each other nervously.

"Get down. All of ya's get down," said Johnny. He spoke in a calm and detached manner. Yet none of them doubted there would be hell to pay if they didn't follow this order. As the boys quickly hugged the ice with their stomachs, their conversation grew fever pitched.

"You don't think that sonofabitch is comin' out here?" Tappy asked.

"Well, I don't know." Big Sal turned to Tappy. "Dere were about a dozen people. Dey had lanterns and sleds and a coupla' big guys had sticks."

"They're gonna beat the shit out of us," Frankie wailed.

"We can take on any Irish!" somebody piped in.

"Not twelve of 'em," Tappy countered.

"Now, wait a minute," Louie said, turning to Big Sal roughly. "First you said there were a coupla guys and some kids wid a sled. Now it's up to twelve big guys wid sticks! You gotta get your story straight before Frankie shits his pants and we find out it's Snow White and the Seven Dwarfs over dere!"

To this, Big Sal spluttered: "I don't know. It was dark—I couldn't see...but it was definitely some guys wid sticks!" he said. "And they had a sled too! I know that!"

"Oh yeah! You know!" Louie answered caustically. "You don't know shit from Shinola!"

"Well, I oughtta..." Big Sal retorted.

"Shut up, all of ya's!" Johnny commanded.

"There were big guys dere, with sticks!" Frankie repeated, to the irritation of everyone else.

And in the midst of all this, the boys heard another "whoosh!", the sound each had made as they glided over the ice earlier.

"What...?" Louie muttered.

And then...

"AAAAAAHHH!!!!!" Frankie's scream pierced the night air. After hearing it, Leo sprang to his feet on the slippery ice with ease. With the same hair trigger reflex, Johnny and all of Leo's friends jumped out of sight, but Leo was soon made to understand the reason they had scattered.

It was Cohan!

There, about a yard from Leo's feet, was the policeman— attached to a sled and looking like a blanketed mountain!! The cold had turned his cheeks bright red, while his brown eyes bulged frighteningly, and steam escaped his mouth like a hyperactive smokestack. One side of Cohan's face was concealed by the visor on his hat. But the visible part of the policeman's face looked enraged. He had plowed into the group like a luge at an Alpine Olympics.

Like Frankie, the surprise inspired Leonardo to a bloodcurdling scream that joined a chorus of screams that shook the Farms as the boys scattered over its icy plain.

About an hour later, Leonardo's feet touched the familiar cobblestones of Thompson Street. He was running behind Johnny, barely keeping sight of his brother's black felt jacket and an accompanying blur that was Johnny's street cap. Leo's chest felt tight. He was thirsty, and despite the steam that shot out of his mouth with every exhale, he was hot. So hot that driblets of sweat were rolling down his chest, back, and forehead.

As he ran, Leo recalled the events that followed their exit out of the Farms. How the boys had slid, crawled, pulled, and clawed themselves off the ice. How, sure enough, there had been some Irish boys on the ice's edge, waiting for them to come out. And, how, when Leo and his friends finally did come out, they were detained by the group of Irish boys while one of their number went in the Farms to get Cohan.

It was a nightmare from start to finish. Right up to the time Frankie scared off the Irish boys by pretending to have a fit of epilepsy. Leo recognized the ploy, because he had used it himself when he and Frankie met *the* Red *LaRocca* in an alley one day. The trick worked, with the Irish reacting like blindfolded banshees, buying Leo, his friends, and Johnny enough time to get out of harm's way.

Now, Leo's only thought was to get home. Nonetheless, he would have run straight past 101 Thompson Street if a hand didn't grab his arm and pull him into the building roughly.

Leo looked at the hand clutching his coat sleeve. He saw it was attached to the sleeve of a black jacket that his eyes followed to a shoulder, a face—it was Johnny's, he noted thankfully. His brother pushed him to a corner of the tiled lobby. Then Johnny turned again to the doorway, to pull Tappy and Big Sal inside, before shutting the door.

"I don't know where Louie and Frankie are, but Cohan's comin' up Thompson," Johnny said. "Let's get outta here." Leo, Tappy, and Big Sal obediently followed Johnny up four flights of stairs to where he and Leo lived. As it so happened, nobody else was in the apartment. In any case, Cohan was the immediate concern.

The boys filed to the window facing the street.

"Stay away from there!" Leo urged. "Cohan'll see you!"

But Johnny was already there. He pulled the curtain aside to stare out the window, while Leo's friends followed suit. Leo joined them sheepishly.

Cohan had found the building, alright, and was just stepping out the front door, back onto Thompson Street. He turned to face them, and the boys got a good look at the policeman for the first time since he'd marooned himself on the ice of the Farms.

31

Leo gasped. It looked as if Cohan had gone through the wringer on a washing machine. His hat sat on his head backwards, with his hair hanging in clumps on the sides. He glistened with sweat that covered his face and neck and darkened his shirt and chest, and his coat dragged in the back where the hem was ripped.

Maybe he wasn't sure if this was the place where the boys had escaped. Maybe he saw them go into the building but didn't know if they were still inside. In any case, Cohan was eyeballing the structure—mulling over every window and crack in its facade. Inevitably, he caught sight of the boys peering out of the Caraciella flat.

Not knowing what a strange picture he presented, the policeman assumed a look of triumph and mouthed something. Johnny raised the window so they could hear. "You can put it off..." Cohan was saying. "But you have to come down sooner or later."

The boys looked at each other in horror. It was true. Eventually they would have to go down. And when they did, they might be carted off to jail, perhaps to join Frankie and Louie, who could be behind bars already.

Leo fumed. *It's all Johnny's fault!* he told himself. If his brother hadn't gone to the window, Cohan wouldn't be out there now. If Johnny hadn't talked them into building that fire, none of this would have happened! Leo, of course, didn't have the nerve to say any of this. He could only glare at Johnny, afraid to chastise his well-liked brother in public.

Johnny, Tappy, and Big Sal meanwhile began to speculate on how long the policeman would be willing to wait for them. Suddenly, Johnny's face brightened.

He walked back to the window and stuck his head outside. Putting a fist to his mouth, Johnny sounded an enormous Bronx cheer.

The policeman snapped his head towards the window to see Johnny staring at him belligerently. "You're full of shit, we live here!" Johnny shouted. Then he closed the window and turned around.

The boys were silent. Gradually, stirred by shock and relief, they began to giggle. It was as easy as that! Cohan couldn't wait *forever* for them to come down. And it was a good bet he wouldn't run to the station house for reinforcements. What—send in a dozen cops to smoke out four boys who built a bonfire? New York was a metropolis of six million people, most of whom had more serious things to worry about.

The marvelousness of it all inspired the boys to a round of Bronx cheers, hoots, shouts, and rhymes ("Brass buttons, Blue coat/Can't catch a Nanny coat!") they liked so much, they decided to treat Cohan to some of it. But when they hung out the window so the policeman could hear them, they found Cohan was as tickled as they were. Bent beneath the window, the man was retching howls of delight, brought on, it seemed, by Johnny saying that they lived there.

The boys stopped laughing and looked at each other. They were relieved, though each would rather have died than admit it.

The policeman wasn't angry. That was good. It was also…strange. Who'd of thought Cohan could like a joke on himself?

"I told you he flipped his lid," Johnny muttered. He closed the window and turned around, somehow disturbed by the evening's outcome.

Only Leo wasn't surprised by Cohan's behavior. There were sides and shades to the policeman Leo's friends didn't know about, stories they'd never believe even if he tried to tell them. Which is why he never did.

In a few minutes Cohan was gone, and Tappy and Big Sal left for home.

After this incident, Leonardo began to see Cohan in a different way. He realized the policeman knew what it was like growing up on the streets. He was from somewhere around there, for Christ's sake, and probably remembered what it was like to be a kid. So, naturally, he understood about bonfires and poker games and playing tricks on coppers.

And whether he was Irish, or Jewish, it really made no difference. Not to Leo it didn't. Cohan had always treated him okay. There were the times he belted him on the shoulder, but he did that to everyone, the Irish and Jewish kids included. And he was a cop, sure—but so what? They weren't all bad, no matter what Johnny said. (And who was Johnny to say what was good or bad?)

Not that Leo wasn't scared for a few days. Afraid Cohan would come around with the paddy wagon and take them all away, he started taking a new route to school, ducking into alleys and behind newspaper stands when he thought he saw a Navy coat in the crowd. He invented ailments and other excuses to avoid running errands for his mother and went straight home after school. In short, he stayed away from everybody and everything, so Cohan wouldn't have clues as to his whereabouts.

Nonetheless, Leo did run into Frankie one day, in the hallway of their building. Frankie's head was wrapped in a strip of bedding beneath his street cap.

Leo had been wondering what happened to his friend, and was relieved to find he was okay, though wounded. "Did those Irish bastards do this to you?" he demanded. "If they did, I'll kill 'em, Frankie."

"No." Frankie answered. "I got 'dis havin' my eckilepdic fit—and boy did it hurt. It ain't no wonder them guys Nab-Leon and Jellius Caesar acted so crazy, wantin' to take over the world. A coupla' dese tings and you'll knock every brain you got outta your skull. I had it wid bein' an eckilepdic. No more a' dat stuff for me."

Leonardo was so glad to see Frankie, he decided not to correct his pronunciation or opinion of Leo's heroes. Instead, he listened to how Frankie hid inside a Sixth Avenue movie theater after running from the Irish kids, staying there until it was safe to go home. In turn, Leo told Frankie everything that happened to him, Johnny, Tappy, Big Sal, and Cohan. Then, the two vowed to keep out of sight until they knew Cohan wasn't holding any grudges and, using their own special blood brother salute, said "good-bye."

But all these efforts turned out to be for nothing. Cohan finally caught up with Leonardo while he was behind *Delvecchio's* Bathhouse, reading "An American Tragedy."

It was less than a week after the bonfire incident, and the first time Leo let down his guard in five days. Now, enjoying the steam floating from the open windows of the bathhouse, Leo tried to be casual, even as the men who stumbled out of *Delvecchio's* back door stared, puzzled by his choice of a place to read.

Leo saw Cohan's shadow before he heard his voice. It was huge and imposing, blocking the sun as it dropped for the evening.

"There you are!" The policeman boomed.

The effect of this statement was well calculated. Leonardo didn't disappoint Cohan with his reaction. First, he threw his book in the air. Then, he bounced, landing on the ground gracelessly.

The embarrassment this caused to Leo was punctuated by Cohan's gravelly laugh. Not the hysterical laugh from the night of the bonfire, but a hearty, raucous laugh. The kind to be expected from a man who likes a good joke—especially one on himself.

Leo rose to his feet, barely able to make eye contact with the policeman. Cohan walked around him, enjoying the tremors rippling Leo's spine.

"So...you found a new reading spot, eh?" Cohan looked at Leo severely.

Leo nodded. Because his body was shaking so, his arms and torso followed his head up and down.

"What's wrong with the old spot? Too popular with the other bookworms?" Cohan asked.

To this, Leonardo shook his head from side to side, and again, his body followed the motion of his head. Cohan had to chuckle.

"You wouldn't be avoiding me—wouldja?" and he made a move to slap Leo's shoulder. Beside himself with terror, Leo looked as if he would faint before Cohan could come near to touching him.

The policeman's laughter was softer now: "Hey, I'm just kiddin' with you." To prove it, he patted the boy's shoulder gently.

"Just promise me one thing." Folding his arm around the boy's shoulders, he looked straight and evenly into Leo's eyes. "No more bonfires."

Leo nodded. This was an easy promise to make. It was days ago, while Cohan was chasing them down McDougal, that Leonardo had decided he'd never so much as light a candle again.

The conversation turned to other things—Leo's grades and the coming holidays, the weather and the joys of Jack Armstrong novels and poker on the sidewalks. By the time Cohan took leave of Leonardo, the boy was secure in the knowledge there'd be no retaliation for the other night. He also felt—just a little—like Cohan had become something of a friend.

But this was a crazy thought for a kid to have about a policeman, and Leo pushed it to the back of his mind. Then he ran off to tell Frankie life was back to normal.

ROSALIA'S REVENGE

They first saw each other on the platform. The *Baronessa*, dressed in a brown street coat with fur collar, a turban on her well-groomed head. And Rosalia, wrapped against the cold as best she could manage. Both from *Centuripe*, Sicily.

Rosalia's jowls were unrisen bread dough; the shadows round her eyes, bruises on fruit. Her head was mostly white, save a few black hairs that clung to their youthful state stubbornly. By contrast, the *Baronessa's* face was all soft grooves and muted lines, her hair dyed a tasteful auburn.

The two women did not acknowledge each other. The time for doing so passed the moment the *Baronessa* stepped on the platform, looking straight ahead. Once aware of her presence, Rosalia became awash in fear and resentment, emotions buried so deeply in history, she thought their cause was the cigar being puffed by the man standing next to her.

Rosalia herself stood beneath the sign for Track Five, the track she hoped would soon deliver a train to take her to the Veteran's Hospital in Sheep's Head Bay. There, her son, recently admitted after being injured in the war across the ocean, awaited her visit. Unfamiliar with her surroundings, Rosalia clung to that sign like a bird in sight of a nourishing worm. Like a bird, moreover, who was afraid her only meal in days would be snatched away.

Everything about the subway startled Rosalia. First, the way the trains screeched as they pulled into the station, then, the relentless pace of the rush hour commuters, packed together like ants on the crest of an anthill. She was equally alarmed by the platform uniting token booths and train tracks, the tunnels and signals, the turnstiles and escalators seeming to devour the crowd one person at a time. She cringed at the sound of the loudspeaker, afraid of the loud, choppy rhythm of the announcer's voice, and equally terrified the words she could not understand would announce her train without her knowing it.

And here, of all places, was the *Baronessa*.

When a train did come up Track Five, it growled to a halt that sent Rosalia beneath the shelter of her own upraised arms. Cautiously eyeing the train's exterior, she saw it was almost as marked and distressed as the ancient ruins in her native land, yet was pleased to see the interior had some empty seats. How she would relish putting her aching back into one of them. Still, she was uncertain the iron serpent before her was the train she needed to board.

Beyond a doubt she was in the King's Highway subway station. That much she'd seen on the sign outside the station, even though she could not read—not English or her native Sicilian. The tiny woman left her family's Brooklyn brownstone to shop, go to church, or visit relatives only, and had a great fear of going out in the world alone. That's why her daughter rehearsed with her how to find the local subway before she set out, going so far as to write the names of the stations where she was to get on and off the train.

Now, Rosalia held onto that scrap of paper as if her life depended on it. KINGS HIGHWAY it said at the top. On coming upon the station, she checked her daughter's jottings once, twice...five times, plunging down the stairs only when thoroughly convinced she was at the right place.

Inside, she walked to the token booth: "Sheep-ahs Ed-uh Bay-uh?"

The clerk glanced at her: "Sheep's Head Bay? Yeah. Track Five."

"*Che dice?*"

The impatient clerk took a pencil and scratched a five on the metal counter. "FIVE," he repeated, pointing to the sign. Rosalia nodded, then walked to the designated area, where she stayed—not moving a muscle—until she set eyes on the *Baronessa*.

Now, a train was before her. And Rosalia was afraid to board it. Not just afraid, but unable to, for her feet were suddenly heavy as concrete.

Lost in her doubts in this way, Rosalia came close to returning home, until a man onboard the train noticed her hesitation.

"Getting on?" he called out.

Rosalia didn't understand. But his polite concern was the anecdote to her confusion. The heaviness in her feet subsided, and she felt herself pulled through the open doors of the train. Slowly at first, then with the accumulated force of a magnet.

Once inside, she quickly sat down, smiling at the nice man who helped her. She thought no more about whether she was on the right train; nor did she think to ask how many stops to the Veteran's Hospital. She was too relieved to have a seat for her aching back. When she was finally settled, she had the surprising notion that riding the subway was almost pleasant. But not quite.

Despite her physical comfort, Rosalia was uneasy about something or someone aboard that train. Slowly, not moving her head or eyes or being obvious, she pieced together what was distracting her. It was the *Baronessa*. Incredible. First, spotting her there in the station, now having her as a fellow passenger on the subway car. It was uncanny, and Rosalia came close to making the sign of the cross. Yet, while she sat rock still, she couldn't help noticing the *Baronessa* gave every sign of knowing of Rosalia's presence, just as Rosalia knew of hers; and she seemed just as unwilling to acknowledge it.

For one thing, though she paced the subway car (presumably to find a seat) the *Baronessa* avoided the end where Rosalia was seated. Moreover, as she walked, her eyes scanned every bench, except Rosalia's.

Well, she could look high and low and use a magnifying glass even, Rosalia mused. She would still find only one empty seat in the car. That was the one directly next to Rosalia. A location where neither Rosalia wanted her, nor, apparently, the *Baronessa* wanted to be. Still, it was no surprise to Rosalia when the other woman ducked into that space as the train started on its rocky course. For though the *Baronessa's* face looked as soft as a pressed rose, Rosalia knew the aristocrat was many years older than she was.

"Ciao, Rosalia," the *Baronessa* said, in her cool, gracious manner.

"*Baronessa*," Rosalia replied.

"It's been a long time." Her speech was like Rosalia's, but woven with the upper-class Italian used by her schoolmates and family in Italy.

Rosalia understood enough to reply: "Si, *Signora* Carluzza. Many years." She kept her eyes low, falling back on the subservience she learned as a girl in Sicily.

"The years have taken their toll on you, as on me. But I still see a great deal of youth in your eyes, Rosalia. How are you and your family?"

Rosalia paused. She was accustomed to talking to the butcher and the peddler, her neighbors while they were doing laundry, the priest at church. Not to ladies in turbans. Yet, no help could be found on the piece of paper that Rosalia clutched tightly in her hand. For this, she was on her own, a realization that set her head to aching.

How could she answer the question? She would never admit the short trip she and her husband had planned to America had turned into thirty years of living only a hand-to-mouth existence. Or that the place they lived now was as far from her native home as Mount *Etna* was from Prospect Parkway.

There had, of course, been happy moments during her time in America. The births of her children. Baptisms, weddings, holy days.

But on this particular day, she saw her life in New York as little more than working and saving, saving and working, all the time looking to her return to Italy, with its olive groves and sheep herds and village churches. But then a sickness, or even the generosity of her husband, who sent ship's passage to their most far-flung relatives, put Rosalia back where she started: desperate to be home, and despairing that she'd ever see it again.

Then came the war. That cataclysm sent her sons to places Rosalia didn't know existed. Seeing all three deployed in the same disheartening week was the only misfortune that could—and did—break her heart. Now, she greeted each day with her newly emerging sentiment for America and the lie it held for the poor and downtrodden: "*Mannagia L'America!*" Damn America! Damn its wars and economic depressions! Damn its lack of protocol, the missing tradition that spelled out chapter and verse of life in Sicily! Damn its soft bread, its hoodlums, its airless houses; its noisy trains, cable cars, and jackhammers. And she'd keep damning it until the day she put herself aboard the vessel that took her home.

How could Rosalia say this to *Signora* Carluzza? Her experience of America would be entirely different from her own, Rosalia was sure. So, she kept her tongue, mindful that in Sicily they used to say those of the *Baronessa's* class worshipped the devil.

Still, both women were intensely curious about the other. This overwhelming curiosity eventually pulled them into conversation, one the *Baronessa* initiated.

"Come Rosalia, tell me! Are you living on one of those streets paved with gold we used to hear about?"

Rosalia looked at her sourly. "We're content that the roads are paved," she replied. She had surprised herself by saying something good about her adopted country.

Signora Carluzza nodded: "You can satisfy yourself with a little. That's a blessing."

Then: "I've learned to be happy with less, Rosalia. My family lost their land. No peasants to work the estate, you understand, and so it became worthless. If the peasants had stayed, we'd be there still."

Rosalia's eyebrows came together in a frown.

"And what of the difficulty finding work here? How have your people managed?" the other woman clucked. "There was always work in Italy—for anyone who could tolerate some hardship."

What do you know about hardship? Rosalia bristled inside herself. It was best, however, to be on good terms with the *Baronessa*. Should her family return to Sicily one day, they wouldn't want *Signora* Carluzza or her family as enemies. The *Baronessa* wanted to know if things had been difficult. Well, things were always difficult, to one degree or another. On this side of the Atlantic they didn't starve—that was the difference.

"Yes, it has been difficult. But here, we do not go hungry."

Rosalia was soon to know this had been a mistake. She realized—too late, course—that she shouldn't have stated a preference for her adopted land to the *Baronessa,* who was quick to retaliate. "How do you like seeing your children fighting their cousins in Italy?" she asked, fiercely.

Rosalia saw that the *Signora* visibly regretted these words as soon as she said them, no doubt because of the hurt that was amply displayed on Rosalia's face. A simple apology might have mended the rift between the seat mates, but *Signora* Carluzza chose instead to turn away, shifting her eyes to the train's blackened windows as it sped through a tunnel between Coney Island and Grave's End.

Her evasiveness allowed Rosalia to gather her wits.

"I wish my boys were home, it's true," she replied, after some minutes.

She was talking to the *Baronessa's* eyebrows, raised, in shock, almost to her hairline. "But I'd rather see them fight and remain free than become slaves—the way the rest of the world has—to the Japanese and Germans, and to Italy."

The thought was something Rosalia overheard her husband saying to their neighbor. What it expressed was not at all contrary to the way they lived. They had left Italy to escape hunger and found freedom from their ancient overlords in the process. Rosalia had a sense, if only a vague, shadowy one, that her sons were continuing the same struggle by being in the war.

Marble-faced, *Signora* Carluzza dropped her eyes from Rosalia's face. In the same manner, she lifted her face to look out the window, now giving a view of rooftops and chimneys as the train ran along an elevated track. All the while keeping her eyes well away from Rosalia, whom she did not look at again until the end of their shared journey.

So they sat, the combination of quiet and the train's rhythm lulling Rosalia almost to sleep, as her head dropped gently from one shoulder to the other.

It was a matter of sheer luck she awoke to see the station signs flashing in the windows as the train pulled into Sheep's Head Bay. She peered down to confirm the signs showed the words her daughter had written. The signs, the paper. Yes, this was her stop.

Convinced she was at her destination, Rosalia's heart began to palpitate. She faced the same terror that had greeted her on every leg of her journey, only more so to think of stepping into a strange, new place where anything could happen. Still, Rosalia told herself she'd get off the train, whatever it took.

This matter resolved, she looked at the *Baronessa* with some remorse. Shortly after their spat, doubts had started to plague her. Even while she drowsed off, she wondered mightily about her husband's reaction if he heard how she had disrespected the *Baronessa*.

Rosalia remembered a precept of her peasant childhood: that every creature in the world had its place and function. It was not in the scheme of things for a peasant to best a *Baronessa*. If only she hadn't lived on this side of the Atlantic for so long, this truth wouldn't have slipped her mind. But something—the air in this New York, probably—made her forget.

Well, she'd make up for it. It was the way of the women in her native village to curtsey to a person of the *Baronessa's* stature. *Signora* Carluzza would be delighted to know Rosalia still knew this courtesy. It would bring the old days, the wonder of those simple times, back to them both.

And so, scrambling to her feet once the train was stopped, Rosalia turned to face *Signora* Carluzza directly. Dipping in the unmistakable gesture of homage, she marveled at how instinctive the gesture was, even for her sciatica-ridden back. But she was even more surprised by the *Baronessa's* look of dismay.

Perhaps fearful what the other passengers would think, or dumbfounded by a sight she hadn't seen in years, *Signora* Carluzza raised a hand to motion Rosalia to stop. When that didn't work, she rose to her feet instantly, urging Rosalia to do the same.

"There's no need for this, Rosalia. You know it isn't done in this country."

"Yes, but *Signora*..." Rosalia began...

"Remember what you said about not being a slave to another," *Signora* Carluzza chided.

That was the moment Rosalia turned her back on dreams of returning to her native land. And the final glance she gave to *Signora* Carluzza, a woman for whom she bore equal parts hatred and reverence and never again would see, was followed by one thought: "*Benedetto L'America*." (God Bless America.)

VITA

Vita's eye caught the shine coming off the man's epaulets as she peered from the balcony of her family's *salotto*. The pale beacon navigated the crumbled stones of *Sant'Agata's* main street, lingering on facades and fountains, the smooth relief of house stones, doorposts, the hammered metal of the balcony where she stood. The sun's rays against the windows of the *salotto* met the stranger's golden lights in the street, and the man, gorgeous in plumes and pressed fabric, turned his head towards her, his eyes nut brown and amber in the unforgiving glare, his patent leather shoes clicking the ground in tacit rhythm with his regiment.

Vita Citterio, daughter of Ignazio, a harness-maker, watched the procession the way she had gazed at the porcelain doll given to her on her twelfth birthday. Never had she seen anything so beautiful. Not the blush on the cheeks of the doll (which she baptized "Desidera") nor its blue eyes, nor the green taffeta providing the perfect counter note to the doll's shiny, black hair. She was the epitome of every beauty Vita had ever known. From the marionettes that graced the stage at Papallo's puppet theater, to the wildflowers, thousands and thousands of them, that emerged every spring, like silk-draped nobles, beneath the old Greek columns framing *Sant'Agata's* northern approach. On this day, Vita saw the same marriage between fantasy and reality in the contingent passing her family's two-story dwelling.

No matter that the clip-clop of these footfalls on *Via della Santa Croce* was tantamount to an invasion, or that the arrival of these troops had forced her brother Carlo to leave *Sant'Agata*. Vita knew only that this parade was a welcome contrast to *Sant'Agata's* tumbled walls and mud-caked streets, to the drab wheat stands that skirted its crests and surrounded its valleys like vultures eyeing its gray isolation.

Ignazio noticed the soldier, too. What impressed him was how the stranger captured his daughter's attention without so much as firing a shot in her direction. Protective of his family's honor, Ignazio grabbed Vita by the waist and dragged her into the house, the way chickens scratching *Sant'Agata's* choked passages were sometimes wrung by the neck. Vita knew better than to squawk like one of those birds. Her mother would do it for her.

"Are we goats, the way you're pushing us through the doors like livestock?" Angiledda Citterio demanded of her husband. Although only Vita was manhandled, the rest of them, her mother, sister, and grandmother, felt the indignity had been visited on themselves.

"Goats!" Ignazio countered. "We would be lucky if people saw us that way. Better that, than to wear the mask on our faces!"

Vita went to a corner of the *salotto*. Although she knew her glance with the soldier caused her father's fury, she perceived—correctly—that the bickering between her parents had little to do with her.

"The mask on our faces!" The tartness in Angiledda's voice would have done justice to the prickly pears that flourished, like bandits, along the mule tracks circling *Sant'Agata*. "What madness is this? My daughter was doing no more than every other girl in *Sant'Agata*! Hasn't enough misfortune visited this family" (here, Angiledda referred to her son's hurried flight) "without your strange imaginings bringing more on us!?"

"It would be better for you to watch your daughter's eyes than my so-called imaginings! There'll be little to imagine when horns sprout on this head," thumbs extended, Ignazio's hands pumped the air in front of his forehead, "—and I reckon with the bitch who put them there!"

"Now I know you've lost your mind!"

At this, Vita left the room to descend the stairway outside the house. She'd pass the remainder of the squabble in her father's storeroom, a silent witness to a pattern as familiar and predictable as the fissures that sank between the stones of *Via della Santa Croce* during the island's hot season.

Her father would be unsparing in his anger, her mother's attempts to reason with him like trying to drain the Sicilian sun from the sky: to sprinkle it deliberately, like an incantation, on olive groves, wheat fields, upon the gypsum hovel of a shepherd family living on *Sant'Agata's* outskirts. (Where, at that very hour, they mumbled over a small vat of ricotta, prayed their goats would have enough water that year to ensure manufacture of another one, blessed their bread before breaking it.) If Angiledda could have broken Ignazio's anger, it would have been like feeling the sun's warmth gradually throughout the year, rather than in one blow during a dry season deprived, like Ignazio's rages, of all reason and mercy.

Vita's mother sometimes bore bruises from her clashes with Ignazio. More often—like the earth's uneasy marriage to the sun—she wore the exhaustion of a spouse frittered to waste by her mate.

The physical and emotional scorching that her mother withstood was something Vita decided years before that she would never tolerate. Shrewd and strong-willed, the young woman learned how to get what she wanted early, and, more importantly, how to preserve her dignity while doing so. She held a stubborn belief that her methods, no matter how duplicitous, were correct. For whatever she set her sights on, Vita saw in her own struggles the grievances that her mother suffered with Ignazio.

For instance, when she wanted a shawl to wear to the *Festa di Sant'Agata*, Vita hid a sack of the semolina the family used to bake their daily bread, then reported the flour as missing to her mother, who suffered agonies before telling her husband about the shortage. After Ignazio handed his wife a few guineas to mill more wheat, Vita secreted them away in a bag of coins she'd saved for months.

Vita believed her behavior was just. She saw her mother deceive Ignazio (who was stingier than the soil) countless times, taking money to buy treats for her children. Likewise, in Vita's mind, it was always the unfairness of others that caused her own behavior. Thus, her personality was shaped as much by her mother's reaction to Ignazio's anger, as it was by his frequent rages.

In early October, a month after the Northern regiment's arrival, Vita's mother was having many more of her frequent headaches, and sent Vita to a faith healer for a headache charm. Vita was happy to do it. More and more, Angelidda was asking her to run errands most people would judge unseemly for a young, single woman to perform alone. Angelidda knew her husband would have her skin if he found out. But instead of trying to explain her options to a man with the understanding of a mule, Angiledda took her chances by enlisting her daughter's help.

This is the time when Angiledda also started the curious habit of closeting herself with her daughter-in-law, Nora, in the kitchen or master bedroom for hours when Ignazio was away. What the women discussed, or why they behaved like nuns who had taken a vow of silence when she came in the room, Vita couldn't say. She knew only she was suddenly milling the wheat, buying from peddlers, even braving the soldiers at Carlo and Nora's house to get her sister-in-law's belongings. And while she took a chaperone, usually her six-year-old sister, Maria, with her on these errands, Vita was enjoying a freedom she never before had known.

The old charm healer, *Zia* Galorma, was as wrinkled and brown as the olives drying in the sun on the heels of the harvest. She lived in a hut across from *San Calogero*, an abandoned monastery on the town's eastern flank. This is where the Northern soldiers stayed during the town's occupation, trailing cigarette butts, empty wine bottles, and offensive remarks about their Sicilian hosts to pass the time. These comments were heard with little more than suspicion, for the Italian they spoke was as incomprehensible to the people of *Sant'Agata* as their habit of carrying their daily wastes to a pit outside the town.

While Maria chased the holy woman's cats in the yard, Vita sat inside *Zia* Gilorma's hut. Having been assured by Carlo that much of what passed for medical knowledge in *Sant'Agata* was superstition, Vita had little interest in the faith healer's remedies, and looked hard at the gloves on her hands to keep her eyes off the concoction being prepared. *Zia* Galorma sensed her discomfort.

"You overreach yourself, with your hats and gloves," she chided. These were, indeed, unusual attire for an artisan's daughter. "I know a wealthy peasant who would be happy to marry a harness-maker's daughter *who knows her place.*" *Zia* Galorma made her living partly as a matchmaker.

"Be quiet," Vita hissed. Her low regard for *Zia* Gilorma was enhanced by her view of the monastery from the window of the hut. This, the faith healer noticed, too.

"Nothing like a soldier to set a young woman's veins on fire," she said. "You should be careful, looking at them the way that you do..."

Vita backed up, much like a rearing mule, to protest.

"Still, with the proper charm they can be managed. See me if you need one," *Zia* Galorma finished. Vita snatched the charm bottle from the woman's hands and marched out of the hut.

The thought of being involved with one of the foreign soldiers made Vita feel sick. So much, that she didn't give the monastery a second glance. As a result, she failed to see that the soldier who caught her eye on the day of the incursion was just then staring at her from the front of the monastery, buttoning his jacket, smoothing his hair. But by the time he'd performed these niceties, Vita had collected her sister and left.

In the days to come, Vita's errand-running reached a fevered pitch. Instead of walking the main road, where neighbors could see her, Vita and her sister rounded the village's east flank, steering away from the business district until they were just short of *Sant'Agata's* gate, the tops of the Greek columns guiding their way. From there, they picked up a narrow mule path that followed the city wall. A thousand veins leading to every point in *Sant'Agata* shot off this artery. Though most were overgrown with foliage and slick with manure, they took Vita where she needed to go, and also protected her from the gossip of neighbors who'd be shocked by the freedom with which she traversed the local environs.

While this ancient track was much more difficult to walk than the road, Vita noticed there were others who preferred it as much as she. And it was no surprise, of course, when she stumbled across the Northern soldiers walking the track, for they naturally wished to avoid being taunted by the people of *Sant'Agata*. More puzzling was how often she came face-to-face with the particular soldier: the tall one with the nut-brown eyes who had exuded such glory on the day the soldiers came to town. At these times, Vita conducted herself as any self-respecting girl would. She ignored him. And he did not greet her. Yet, their paths crossed often enough for Vita to wonder if, due to her behavior towards the faith healer, she had been made the target of one of the woman's curses.

One morning a few days later, Vita and Maria walked to the town's *panificcio,* and, for the first time since the summer riots, found it delightful to stick their heads inside the short doorway. Vita's nose and eyes became infatuated with the crusty, golden loaves piled in every corner, hanging in nets from the plaster-coated ceiling, tantalizing in their dual-aroma of poppy seeds and yeast.

On entering this day, however, Vita's senses were assailed by more than bread. For, next to the pay table, just having left a coin with the baker's wife, stood the tall, handsome, Northern soldier.

His arms and those of his companion were filled with bread. Enough, thought Vita, to feed the entire contingent of Northern soldiers. Yet, the loaves, whose pointy ends covered the bottom of his face and surely drove him crazy with their aroma, didn't stop the young man from taking blatant notice of her. So much so that Vita looked away as he walked to the door.

Vita wasted no time leaving the shop when her business was finished, her hands trembling round the bundle she held in her arms. Less obvious was how her knees wobbled beneath her skirts just before she collapsed to sit on the ledge of the city fountain, as Maria drew near.

Just at this moment, a small boy approached them.

"What is your name, *Signorina*?" the boy asked Vita, as he took her measure with his large, hazel eyes. Vita mumbled incoherently to the ground. But the boy didn't wait for her answer. Instead, he pressed her hand, then darted away like a jackrabbit.

Vita looked down to find a piece of paper in her palm. She unfolded it slowly and read: *I love you. Meet me behind the vineyard of the old monastery after sunset.*

Frantically, she looked around. Her eyes soon found the handsome Northerner, free now of his burden of bread, standing at the opposite end of the piazza. His companion nowhere in sight, the smile the soldier bestowed on Vita melted her heart, while the expression in his eyes filled her with warmth. Finally, the man inclined his head as if to say, "Well then," and he was gone.

It happened so briefly, Vita wondered if she imagined it, yet in the same split second, she decided to keep the proposed rendezvous, admitting to herself she'd been looking at the soldier with heart's eyes for some time. Of course, the fact that he was a foreigner, part of an occupying force, no less, hadn't allowed her to consider him a potential suitor. But now—like the happy shock of the land receiving its first rain after the dry season—Vita saw the opportunity for what it was: A chance to have the thing she wanted more than anything.

She had natural misgivings about meeting a stranger, alone, at night. But the liberty given to her over the past months had ended inhibitions that were once second nature to her. While she knew consenting to the meeting put her reputation at risk, the chance to have the glamorous stranger to herself, for a moment or an hour, was something she could not pass up. Influencing her decision in no small way was the example of her mother, whose life showed Vita the approval of relatives and neighbors was little comfort when one lacked happiness. Of course, it helped that when she was small, she had a doll named Desidera—giving her a taste of what it was like to want something with all her might, and then receive her heart's desire.

And so, much later, when her sister's breathing slowed to a trickle, Vita crawled from their bed, walking with a snail's step through the darkened house. Ignazio had taken noisy leave of his family hours before and would not be home for weeks. As for her mother, Angelidda was once more shut inside the kitchen, talking with her daughter-in-law.

Outside, Vita blessed the night for lending her its black veil, a garment she would wear often in the weeks to come. The kerosene lamp in the kitchen spilled light between the window and the shutter—an insipid glow compared to the not quite full moon. When Vita set foot on the mule path, its layer of pig manure and vines made her shoes slide, as it did in the day. But tonight, her disgust for this sensation was replaced by an awareness of how her breath rose with every step, the way it did when she walked down the aisle in church.

There would be no priest to perform sacred mysteries on a linened altar at the end of this night's journey. But there would be mystery, in the guise of the soldier. A man who was a foreigner, whose name was unknown to her, but whose face was as dear to her as her parents and the neighbors and relatives she'd known since she was a child. And the odor coming off the track was not of shit and rot, but of a clean-shaven face, dozens of semolina loaves, and the slight aroma of tobacco she smelled on him that distant morning, in that far-away bakery, at the beginning of that incredibly long day.

So, when she met the soldier, whose name was Stephano, she felt what passed between them had been destined to happen just as it did, that very night, beneath the tangled grape vines. And by sunrise, when the sun chased away the moon, Vita had no doubt her fate was permanently joined to his. Nor could she doubt he felt the same way about her.

Angiledda nearly walked into her daughter when Vita came through the door the next morning. Fortunately, Vita had fetched a sack of flour from the storeroom before going in the house. She hoped her mother would believe she'd been up earlier than the rest of the family (and this much was true), to take some wheat to the miller.

The ploy worked. But then again, Vita thought any excuse would have served to explain her whereabouts on this morning. Angiledda's eyes were shadowed. By worry, Vita was certain, and from being too close to the smoke of the kerosene lamp all night.

"What is it, Mama?" Vita asked.

Angiledda's words sputtered, and the woman, after a struggle, gave up the effort. Vita turned away. She wasn't interested in her mother's problems, had only asked because it was the thing to do. Her heart beat like a hammer and anvil—muffled, she hoped, by an exhaustion she carried with a kind of radiance. Nonetheless, her tousled hair and wrinkled clothes were clues of where she was night before, and Vita wanted to remove them from her mother's sight before she came to her senses.

As if reading her mind, Angiledda clasped Vita's shoulders to bury her face in Vita's neck suddenly. Alarmed by the gesture, but concerned, too, the pale taste of the soldier's kisses would be discernable, Vita pushed her away.

Angiledda brought her gaze eye to eye with her daughter's, ready now to say what was on her mind.

"Forgive me."

"For what?" Vita couldn't fail to see the irony in her mother's words. It was she who needed forgiveness…even if she had no desire to gain it.

Angiledda turned away. "The mule driver was here last night."

Not knowing what else to make of this statement, Vita wondered if the mule driver had spied on her during the night and told her mother where and with whom she had been. Fearful now, she gasped.

The game is up, Vita thought. *She knows.*

"The mule driver was here to deliver a letter from your brother," said Angiledda. Vita blushed, remembering her thoughts moments before.

"Carlo?" Vita asked.

"Yes, Carlo!" Her mother's arms clamped hers so tightly, tears came to Vita's eyes. "He's in New York! He's safe! And you and Nora and my dearest grandchild are going to join him!"

A native sneakiness made many of Vita's reactions seem passive in that village of loud talkers and hand gesturers. The ache behind her eyes further aided Vita in hiding her feelings. Angiledda took her blank look for shock.

"Yes, yes, my child!" Angiledda's hands crept around Vita's face. "It's a surprise…I know. But you'll like New York. Giuseppe, your uncle… promises to find a husband for you…"

Vita startled her mother with sudden alertness. She pulled away to stare at Angiledda with what the older woman should have recognized as defiance.

"You'll like it," her mother nodded. Vita did an about-face with the intention of making straight to bed.

"Does Papa know about this?" she asked, walking away.

"No...no, Vita! And you must never tell him! Not until the Second Coming...maybe not then!" Her mother pleaded.

Nodding, Vita went to her room.

Hours in her bed brought Vita to terms with her situation. She had no intention of going to New York. But the expectation she would leave Sant' Agata would make the events that were destined to play out easier for everybody involved.

The listlessness Vita exhibited over the next few days caused her mother little concern. The child was in shock, Angiledda told herself. She would leave her family, her home, perhaps forever. She herself had cried over the prospect. But Nora couldn't cross the ocean with only an infant for company. A woman on her own was always a temptation to men and fate. Vita might be able to return, some day in the distant future.

Of course, the way things were going, it might be best to stay away. For this, they had Carlo and his political activities to thank. Yet, Angiledda found it difficult to place any kind of blame on her oldest and only male child. Things had been going this way for a while. Carlo and his cohorts were no more than the match that lit an ever-present fuse.

When Vita told Stephano her mother planned to send her off to New York, he was ecstatic.

"This is perfect," he said to her in the tongue of the Turks. It was a language she had been raised to hate, but now, coming from her beloved, sounded to her like the singing of angels. To be sure, communication was a challenge for them. But since they spent little of their time talking, the difficulty was minor. It was lessened by the few Sicilian words Stephano had managed to learn and the Italian phrases Vita knew from Carlo.

"My commission is nearing its end." They stood outside *San Calogero*, on the side away from the faith healer's hut. "Once I leave the army, we can depart this place and live on my uncle's farm in *Capua*. We won't have much money…but, who knows?" Stephano threw his cigarette in the dust. "Maybe my uncle will give me work. He's getting old, his son is no good." He shrugged. "Maybe I'll get his estate. Would you like that, *carissima*?"

Vita nodded. She came close to saying if they lived in a ditch on the side of the road, she'd be happy. But she had little time for sentiments that didn't satisfy her ends. They were going away together, exactly what she wanted. Still, Stephano hadn't talked about marriage. While in truth it was something Vita could do without, she knew of no other way to attach the young man to herself.

"You see things as I do." And Vita looked alternately at the ground and the walls of the monastery as she spoke. "There is something else I must tell you …"

"Of course, *bellissima*…whatever you wish…"

"Well, certainly it can be no surprise …" and now, Vita became so caught up in the part she was playing, she behaved the way she would if the words she was about to utter were true. That is, she blushed. This was astonishing to Stephano, who'd never seen her face color this way before, even while she was in far more compromising positions. "I'm having a baby."

The disbelief on his face was immediate. It was so obvious, Vita wanted to ask if he knew how babies were made. Unknown to her, it was his mastery of the subject that pressed his skepticism. For Stephano had taken care to make sure a pregnancy didn't occur. His greater experience and (what is more) craftiness cast shame on her own efforts at the same, leaving Vita feeling somewhat ridiculous, while unable to put her finger on why.

Stephano's eyes left her face and fell to the ground. "What shall we do, *carissima*?" She told herself it was not mockery she heard in his voice. And if it seemed unusual for him to ask her to take the lead in so important a matter, well, it was because it was quite unusual for men to give the lead to women, *except* at such times.

"We'll have to marry," she told him.

He nodded, his eyes still downcast.

"My sister-in-law is leaving for Naples in a few weeks. I'll go with her. We can meet at the dock for the Imperial Shipping Line. I can write my mother when we get to…to…."

Vita thanked her lucky stars and the saints in Paradise when Stephano came to her rescue, saying, "My uncle's estate in Capua."

"Yes." She beamed.

Vita, Nora, and the baby stayed four days and three nights at the Imperial Shipping Line hostel in Naples before arrival of the steamboat that would take them from Italy. They stayed in the women's dormer, where the days of waiting were endless for Vita. While Nora was preoccupied with little Carlo, nursing him, shushing him, keeping him entertained, Vita endlessly rehearsed in her head the escape plan she and Stephano had devised before they parted.

He would signal to her from behind the embarkation point, just before the passengers boarded the steamer, waving his red cummerbund among the relatives and friends gathered to say good-bye. That's when Vita would tell Nora she would have to cross the ocean without her—a disclosure that would, naturally, be very upsetting.

Nonetheless, Vita would turn about face on the ship's gangplank, if need be, but not before telling Nora she was destined for a higher calling than being a nursemaid to her brother's family. And it was the speed of the reversal that would assure her escape. She and Stephano thought Vita's defection just

68

before boarding the steamer would prevent Nora from canceling her own ocean crossing. For the couple needed Nora to take the two-week journey to America to give them time to marry and settle in *Capua* before Vita's family could find them.

The particulars of an ocean-crossing were known to Vita and Nora. Both had heard Carlo describe his previous journeys to North America. Nora, Vita was convinced, would not be spared the sea sickness suffered by many, and would likely be unable to leave the steerage hold for the better part of the voyage.

As for herself, Vita was certain she wouldn't have been so beset. She would have been on deck every day, relishing the fresh, open air and the distance between her ocean pedestal and her former buried state in *Sant'Agata*.

Yet, as enjoyable as her impression of freedom might be on the open sea, her captivity would continue in the end. For, in New York, within a tight circle of family and friends, she would continue to be daughter of Ignazio, harness-maker. The same puppet masters would have command of the strings that Stephano alone had the power to sever. Because only his jarring glamour—his looks and charm—could unearth her from the worn, familiar soil where her existence had been sown generations before.

Before their painstaking plans could come to fruition, however, she had to endure waiting in the drab hostel. Four days until Stephano came! He had told her he knew where the Imperial Shipping Line was in Naples, was acquainted with the pier. There was nothing to do but while away the hours, rehearsing her part in the planned betrayal of her sister-in-law and nephew. And the wait to turn her plans into reality was more painful than anything in Vita's life so far.

Preoccupied in this way, Vita was barely civil to the country doctor who befriended the two women by telling them stories of his other voyages. "Before you go on the ship," he said, "a doctor will examine your eyes with a hook. Don't let him. When they did it to me, my eye fell in my pocket."

His and Nora's laughter helped Vita to realize he was joking. But instead of joining in their frivolity, she walked away to tickle little Carlo. Nora and the doctor began talking like friends who had known each other for years. Vita's face was expressionless while she listened.

"You are from *Sant'Agata, Signora*?" asked the doctor.

"*Si*. How did you know?"

"I saw you praying at the little shrine in the alley—the one to *Sant'Agata*. Your ardor gave you away. My brother is the doctor in *San Sebastiano*."

Nora shuddered. "Ah...*San Sebastiano*, in the valley below us. All its people are malarial. It is a place, we say, cursed by God."

"Yes...yes, my brother had the fever last summer," the doctor agreed. "Tell me, *Signora*, what brings you away from your home?"

"My husband is in New York to find work. You've heard about the troubles in Sicily? There's nothing for us there now. "

And there never was, Vita added silently. Tomorrow they, or rather Nora, would board the ship, Stephano would take her away, and the prospect of going back to *Sant'Agata* would be forever removed from her horizon. Only a few more hours, and her real life would begin.

Early next morning, a steamship's whistle rolled them out of bed, while mist hid the view from the hostel's windows. When the mist subsided, Vita saw the moon clung to its place in the gray sky. Forgetting she wasn't going on the ship, she looked in horror at the contrast between the yellow orb and the clouds bedazzling it, thinking what she saw signaled a coming storm. Only later, when the sun broke through the dark veils and evaporated them, did Vita know she was wrong. But this realization, as the morning wore on, was long in coming.

In the meantime, Vita enjoyed the final preparations for the ocean voyage she would not be making. After breakfast, she and Nora went to the apothecary and the city market to buy medical and foodstuffs. Once returned to the hostel, they bathed themselves and the baby, then repacked and arranged their clothing so they could carry as many of their possessions as possible.

She did it all with relish, even knowing some preparations would burden Nora when they parted. For the baby's diapers hung from Vita's petticoat, and half their money was in her corset. Other requisites were in her trunk, which Vita planned to take away with her. Yet she refused to dwell on the hardships her sister-in-law would face in the days ahead. Nora's misery would pale compared to her own joy at being reunited with her lover.

When Vita first started to wonder if Stephano would come, Nora and the baby were still at the hostel, undergoing the physical exam the country doctor had mentioned. Stephano was supposed to arrive just before the ship's departure. Now the steamship was bellowing its final blasts to signal passengers and crew to come onboard. Still, he did not appear. Vita backed away from the pier to try to spot him. But even from this new vantage point, she could not see him.

The idea *'He's not coming'* grazed her mind. It was a thought as remarkable, in its way, as the fact that he had taken so many pains to capture her attention and sustain it for all the weeks they were together. Yet, it entered her head increasingly, until it was as real as the red shell of the *Machiavelli* itself, bouncing on the water, engrossing her as though the world began and ended in its iron frame.

This, then, is my fate, thought Vita. She would never reveal the depth of her humiliation. And she hoped anyone who saw the tears on her face would think they were caused by the gusts volleying the great ship's hull.

Vita saw the steamer with new eyes now. Whereas, not an hour ago, she hated the thought of stepping on it, she now equally hated the idea of staying ashore, embracing the escape from disgrace and Ignazio's rages the ship permitted for her.

It was soon after Vita reached this new plateau of understanding that she saw her sister-in-law running to her across the pier, holding little Carlo.

"We can't go!" Nora stammered. Vita saw that Nora had been eluding the doctor and nurse who carried out the exams, along with two other men who worked for the steamship line. In a matter of seconds, all of them stood beside Vita.

"What are you talking about?" Vita demanded.

Nora held the baby more closely, while trying to wipe away the tears that fell down her face.

"Your sister..." one of the steam line officials began...

"Sister-in-law..." Vita corrected him.

"Your sister-in-law failed the physical for passengers ticketed for an Atlantic crossing. She has trachoma. She can't leave Italy."

Vita scowled. *Well, for heaven's sake.* She thought of the little country doctor's amusing comments the day before. *Far better,* she couldn't help thinking, *for Nora to have lost her eye.*

The company official pressed his nose to a piece of paper thickly inked with names. *"Signora...."* Nora, Vita, and the doctor helped the struggling official: "Citterio."

"Ah...Citterio...that's right," he said. "*Signora* Citterio will receive a full refund of her passage, as will you..." here his eyes skimmed Vita's face "...excluding room and board for three days and nights at the Imperial line hostel..."

"What?" Vita asked sharply.

The company man looked at Vita over the frames of his glasses. "*Signorina*, you must pay for your food and lodging at the hostel. The line would go out of business..."

"You can keep your money!" Vita snapped.

Now it was Nora's turn for confutation. "If they keep our money, we won't be able to buy train tickets home."

"*Sant' Agata*," Vita replied, her voice low and even, "is no longer my home."

Vita wasn't surprised Nora cried on boarding the train out of Naples. This, despite the goodness of the country doctor, who postponed his own ocean voyage to speed her journey with his kind farewells. Soot covered the window where she sat with the baby, depriving her of a view all the way to Messina. Not that it made a difference, for her future was as unclear as her view had been. Still, Nora's nerves were mostly settled when the time came to board the ferry for Sicily.

Vita put her mother's letter describing Nora's journey home into her pocket. There was plenty of time to revisit its sad lines. Perhaps, when her brother returned from work, he could help her compose a reply. She did, however, have her own future to think about, and her fate, while not so well known as Nora's misfortunes, had taken many twists of its own.

Nora had cried for a good many miles of her journey after they parted on the pier of the Imperial Shipping Line. Not Vita. She had been on the deck of the *Machiavelli* every day, enjoying every opportunity to marvel at the magnificent Atlantic plain. Her wonder at the way it could, with dramatic simplicity, both divide and unite, filled her with awe, like the sunrises she never failed to view from the deck each morning.

Recalling her ocean-going experience from Carlo's fire escape, a place not unlike the ship's latch ways, Vita imagined she was back at sea. The feeling was greatly enhanced when a gust of wind shook the fire escape roughly. Undaunted, Vita breathed heavy gulps of the new air.

Then—not unlike a seagull—she laughed.

PAOLO VISITS THE BARON

Mungibeddu was rumbling. There was no mistaking it. A second's blurring of the landscape, a vague loss of balance, the seesawing of tree limbs, eucalyptus and carob, cypress and mimosa; the oscillation of scrub brush and ground cover, exposing where green was cutting away to yellow under the sun's razor. Then, a neat curtsey of hillsides and village, orange and almond groves above, wheat fields below, the milky crest of *Mungibeddu* swaying, capping everything like a disoriented Zeus looking down from Olympus.

Paolo ignored it. He knew the dangers presented by the smoking mountain. He'd seen mudslides and sinkholes, lava paths, ash-shrouded livestock. *Mungibeddu* was his constant companion, and he was aware of its many moods: the difference in the volcano's primitive vocabulary between a case of heartburn and acute appendicitis. Today, she was belching. A little air in the pipes, and who among us (as Paolo's grandfather would say) has not suffered the same?

Paolo smiled at his grandfather's imagined commentary. This, as he tripped on an outcropping of rock and slid headfirst to earth. He landed under the long, spikey stems of an acanthus plant, was rewarded with an alluring glimpse beneath its pink and white flowers. Paolo's lungs filled with dust, his nostrils with the scent of these flowers, flourishing near a well-concealed spring.

Paolo frowned at the rhythmic gurgling of water. In less than a month, it would be gone. Dried up like ocean foam. In fewer than four weeks, all of it—eucalyptus and carob, scrub brush and wildflowers—would wither, casualties of the ongoing drought. This, Paolo knew as truly as he did that Sicily was the apex of the civilized world. For five years (since he was nine) nature had cast her thirsty spell on the land, and nobody expected it to end soon.

So, Paolo approached his village of *Centuripe* with the step of one who lacks purpose. The month was May, when the village usually began the wheat harvest. With the drought, however, wheat was scarce, and the season's frenetic activity was reduced to a trickle. Instead of cutting their staple, the villagers were putting their energies into the broad bean crop, an activity Paolo was excluded from as too many workers jostled for places in the fields.

This year, Paolo's grandfather would harvest the broad beans. Paolo's job was to gather greens for his mother's stewpot. A bag tied around his waist held the cache from Paolo's day of scavenging, a cache that would be increasingly meager in the days to come, as the sun sucked more and more moisture from the exposed earth below.

Recognizing the outskirts of his village, Paolo dug his shoes into rock, reached up and hoisted himself onto a mule track. Here, he could see the panorama of *Centuripe* and its surrounding countryside. It was set on the mountain's western slope with earthiness and majesty, like a sparrow perched on a Greek column. Above was *Mungibeddu*, purple and grey beneath a mantle of white. Below, a twisting, turning descent to the *Simeto* River Valley, an odyssey relieved by tapestries of olive and orange trees, terraced wheat fields, arches of cypress, mulberry, pine, and the occasional flowering Judas, red stains on an otherwise green and gold carpet.

The town itself was a tiered triumph, three stories, balconies from which inhabitants took for granted their God's-eye view of mountain and valley, sky, and water. It was surrounded by a light brown ribbon that crisscrossed the landscape, something the locals sardonically referred to as a "road." Paolo placed his feet on this anomaly to proceed to a house on *Centuripe's* bottom tier.

Here, Paolo saw an old man, bent like a grapevine, stirring a pot over a fire. A man who was indiscernible from his surroundings. His worn street cap and homespun clothes bled into the rough exterior, sometimes gray, sometimes brown under the sun's shifting gaze, of the house behind him. His dusty shoes looked like stones unearthed from the rocky path encircling the house, a path that ran past the black doorway, on to the next house, and the next, connecting these buildings like rosary beads. He blended with twigs, puddles, offal, ruts in the ground. And he and this drab, clay scene contrasted with the jewel tones of the valley.

Paolo walked up to the man, ignoring flies and gnats on the breeze.

"*Ciao*, grandfather," he murmured.

The old man jerked his head, scooping Paolo up from the corner of his eye while continuing the task before him. Paolo loosened the tie around his waist, allowing his canvas bag to drop, and the old man set to work, cutting, washing, muttering about the poor quality of the greens as he tossed them into the pot. Paolo picked up some wood and pushed a couple of frayed, splintered twigs under the pot while surveying the progress of the noon meal.

Gnats blew into his face. These, and ashes from the fire. When they began to sting his eyes, Paolo's grandfather spoke: "You should have gotten here sooner."

Paolo bowed his head.

"How does it go with the wheat?"

Paolo brushed a gnat out from under his collar. "The same," he said. "There is no work for the boys. It's all for the men." He shrugged: a gesture as apathetic as the hills. Paolo tossed more twigs under the pot, and his eyes blazed when the wood reignited. The flames went out, and he was back to staring at the pot's dark interior.

The buzzing of gnats interrupted the silence.

"Alright," the old man intoned. "We go to see the baron." With this decision, a measure of tension melted from the air.

The two ate, dipping into a communal plate, savoring with the deliberation of those who do not know when they will eat again. Finally, the greens slurped up, the last crumb of bread in their stomachs, the old man rose to his feet: "*Andiamo.*"

They walked along *Mungibeddu*'s western rise, turning their backs on the stones of the village to traverse vineyards and orchards, then bypassing these local sights for the exotic hues of the wild. The minutes turned into hours. Paolo watched the sun drag towards the horizon, its rays melting into purple-yellow streaks indiscernible from the twisting passes. He spent much of the time trying to envision the baron's house, thinking perhaps it was a castle with moats and minarets, a harem peering from its battlements. And he saw his grandfather become vigorous again, stretching his 60-year-old legs in long strides, recounting stories he usually saved for the holidays on *Centuripe's* plodding calendar.

Of these, Paolo's favorite was about when his father and grandfather met up with a bandit on their way to *Catania* to sell *Centuripe's* almond crop. The bandit fed them bread and olives, then pulled out a gun and demanded their mule.

"You know the people are united now, and you've heard how and why I fight for the liberty of Sicily," he explained. "Because of this, you must understand that I have to take your mule."

"The mule?!" Paolo's grandfather objected. "It's not ours! The village is depending on us...!!"

"What is a village, compared to a nation?"

Paolo's father rose to the occasion, eager to contribute to the cause. "Put away your gun," he intoned. "We give you this mule...willingly...for the glory of Italy." The almonds came off the mule's back, the men embraced, and bandit and mule soon were gone.

Paolo walked beside his grandfather with a festive gait. "Did you see the bandit again?" he asked.

"No. But he was well known in *Centuripe*. The villagers said we were right to give the mule away. Except for the man it belonged to."

"What did he mean, when he said, 'the people are united now?'"

"He meant we are equal to the nobility."

Paolo nodded. His happy mood was subsiding, the hunger pangs in his stomach replacing the vibrations of his grandfather's resonant voice. Just when he began to fear he could go no further, he saw the dim outline of a rough stone wall in the twilight shadows. They passed more vineyards and groves, and Paolo saw clearly that a village had taken shape around them. Their feet echoed on narrow, rock-encrusted streets where listless animals—goats, donkeys, chickens—stood like sentries, and the buildings, quiet as stone, seemed to look at them through darkened windows. The villagers seated outside these houses observed them, too, with eyes as fathomless as *Mungibeddu*'s crater.

Soon Paolo and his grandfather were in the piazza. Here, more villagers were assembled beneath aged facades and sun-washed balconies, being massaged by the cool fingers of evening, just as Paolo knew the people of *Centuripe* were. The women sat modestly, backs turned to the street, eyes sewn to their work while they mended clothes or spun cloth. The children were scattered, exhibiting, like children everywhere, an energy the adults lacked. The men were mostly idle.

Many called to Paolo's grandfather.

"Salvatore Carminu!"

"Salvatore! What brings you to *Sant'Agata*?"

The older man raised his hand to salute these acquaintances. Those who were closest to the pair heard him say: "We've come to see the baron."

Salvatore soon stopped at a two-story house where more men were idling. He embraced and kissed each of them.

"Salvatore!" one of these men exclaimed, "Your grandson is grown up!"

Paolo's grandfather smiled in a way that surprised Paolo. "Uses the scythe like Turrido—already, at fourteen. In the fields he moves like a jackrabbit. I can't keep track of him!" And he moved back and forth in a zigzag to illustrate.

They slapped the youngster on the back: "Just like your father. No better worker in Sicily."

Paolo turned his eyes to the ground. Accustomed to his grandfather's criticism and the frequent sting of his cap, he spoke seldom and softly. Now that he was the focus of so much attention, he thought being in the spotlight was something he could do without. Nonetheless, regard for the grandson honored the grandfather, and Paolo hoped the attentions of these people would place a whisper of approval on Salvatore's face.

This hope was dispelled with a look. Raising his head, Paolo found Salvatore studying him with skepticism. With eyes that said: "Don't get any ideas." And Paolo's heart plummeted.

Soon the two swept up the house's crumbly staircase. At the top, Salvatore opened the door, and they went inside. Walking through the house as if it were his own, Salvatore shouted a woman's name: "Rosaria!"

There seemed to be a startled silence. Then, the house came alive with movement from behind a curtain, and the recipient of Salvatore's command stepped out to run to Paolo and his grandfather. "Papa!!" The woman kissed Salvatore on both cheeks. "What brings you here?! Did you come from *Centuripe*? You been listening to *Mungibeddu*? It's got a stomach ache, eh?"

Nodding his head perfunctorily, Salvatore presented Paolo to the woman. "This is your nephew."

Rosaria embraced Paolo warmly, then stepped back to examine him, taking in his eyes, his brow, his forehead, in a way that was far more clinical than affectionate. Paolo likewise took stock of his aunt. She was clothed in a mud-brown skirt and worn blouse. Her cheekbones were low. Her eyes, large and sunken and kind.

"Paolo!" She declared. "The picture of Turrido!"

Now Rosaria turned to Salvatore.

Paolo saw how his aunt tried to engage her father's eyes, like a jack rabbit looking for an opening in a garden wall. But Salvatore made no attempt to do the same, and Rosaria, with something of an air of defeat, turned her attention to clearing the table in front of them while her father grumbled about the hunger in his stomach and a hole in his shoe. And the two continued this way, Rosaria distracted by her task, Salvatore muttering to the air, until one of the men from outside came in.

This man's entrance endowed Rosaria with a new dignity. She shook out the dish towel in her hands to sit next to him. The two leaned close to look at Salvatore.

"What's the news?" Rosaria asked.

"Not good," answered Salvatore, his eyes planted on the threshold. "There won't be much wheat. Beans..." he shrugged. A shrug involving chin, mouth, shoulders, and torso. "We have those, but who knows for how long? We came to see the baron."

Rosaria found her own place on the wall to penetrate with dark eyes. "Not good," she repeated.

And it was just when Paolo was thinking these people from *Sant'Agata* were a fine lot, sighing and moaning in their despair as deep as the *Simeto* Valley, that Salvatore tore his gaze from the wall, smacked his hands together: "Let's eat!"

The evening took a turn for the better.

After devouring a plate of beans, Paolo was introduced to the men in front of the house. He learned that two were his grandfather's brothers—Giuseppe, the oldest, and Paolo, called *Lu Russu* (the Red) for hair that long ago had turned gray. Two were Giuseppe's sons, large, quiet men. Another was *Lu Russu's* adopted only son, Luigi, known as *Lu Mulu* (the Mule) because he was believed to be illegitimate (or why was he put up for adoption?). Finally, there was Rosaria's husband, Vincenzo, who had joined them inside.

All these men worked the soil. Each owned his plot of land, even *Lu Mulu*. But only a small plot, and not enough to feed their families.

Paolo knew a curious warmth inside himself when his great uncles told their stories, kneaded his shoulders, patted his face and hair. Rosaria's sons, his new friends, bonded with him over whispered stories about a girl from the neighboring ravine as they played cards in the dust near the house. This was much different from *Centuripe*, where Paolo's life was dominated by work and his grandfather's criticism.

"We should be harvesting our wheat, same as *Centuripe*," *Lu Russu* explained, when the talk became somber. He was older than Paolo's grandfather, his eyes rimmed with red. "But we haven't had any for two years. Day laborers like us don't have enough to do. Mostly, we leave the work for the young guys."

"We older fellas go down to the square, play cards for a cup of coffee or a glass of wine," Giuseppe took up where his brother left off. "But when I lose, I hear, 'You Son of a Bitch, you spent all our money gambling,' that's what my wife says. What does she know? We can't afford pasta anyway. So, it's snails and greens for us. Or nothing."

"My son-in-law wants to go to America." This was one of Giuseppe's sons talking. "He'll take my daughter and grandchildren. We have a small vineyard we're gonna sell to buy them ship's passage. Who knows? We might never see them again." He wiped away a tear.

Lu Russu shook his head. "Pretty soon, so many will be gone, there won't be enough to hoe the fields and plant the seed even after we get some rain. Better to live in a pigpen in Sicily than a palace in America. But the young people always think there's something better," he gestured toward the road.

"My namesake, Uncle Luigi, saw this coming long ago," *Lu Mulu* piped in. "He said: 'Let the baron and his family take our place in the fields. They need a change! Think how tired they are, breakin' their asses, watching their almond trees grow!' I remember this," he assured Salvatore, as though expecting little agreement from the others.

Perhaps to *Lu Mulu*'s surprise, the others nodded, while *Lu Russu* shook his head: "Remember, Salvatore, how it was supposed to be? Land for all of us, liberty, lighter taxes. Now they even have a tax on the mules."

"Promises were broken." Salvatore agreed. "But Turrido died bringing in the baron's grapes for the harvest. When they put my son in the ground, the baron said, 'Anything you need, Salvatore, if it's in my power, will be yours.' And don't forget, the baron was with us."

"'Of hats and dangerous roads speak well but stay away from them'," *Lu Russu* persisted. The proverb was a reference to the nobility, "hats," and their lack of concern for the poor. "We mix up our affairs with theirs, and guess who gets the short end of it?"

"I know, Paolo, I know," Salvatore said with tooth-grinding patience. "But I have to try. He was with us. And I told you, he owes me."

Giuseppe joined the conversation abruptly. "You say he owes you—he does! Even more than you know!!" Giuseppe's voice rose in a baritone comparable to *Mungibeddu*'s lowest strains. Paolo observed he was showing himself to be the zealot of the group. "Once for the son you lost harvesting his land. Twice, because your son died on the land that should have been yours.

"I may not know how to read, I may not know how to write, but I know what the tri-colors stand for. And mark my words..." here he pointed a gnarled index finger at his younger brother. "Those things will be ours someday. It may mean your grandson will have to fight for them all over again, but they will be ours."

The men were quiet. Slowly, one or two shouted *"Bravo!"* until all Paolo's uncles and cousins joined in. Soon they were riding a *sirocco* of emotion, one that pulled other villagers into their circle, and the shouts and cheers became louder. They ended up sending Paolo for some wine, so they could drink a toast "to Sicily...to Italy...to the people."

Paolo ran off with his heart pounding. This talk of war and liberty was intoxicating! *Zio* Giuseppe's speech was like the voice of destiny! Paolo felt as if a cannonball had been shot through his veins, spinning him backwards in time. Placing him, by some conjurer's trick, into the shoes of his father: proud, defiant, embracing that bandit of old.

Next day, after a breakfast of bread and wine, Paolo and Salvatore prepared to leave for the baron's house. "Remember to show proper respect to the baron. Call him 'your Excellency' and kiss his hand," Rosaria said to Paolo, just as he was finishing the wine in his cup.

Salvatore overheard these remarks as he was tugging on his shoes.

"That won't be necessary!" he boomed. "Those customs died 30 years ago with my comrades!" Then, for good measure: "You women spend all your time in church, where those priests fill your heads with shit..."

When they departed, Paolo saw that Rosaria's kiss for her father was grudging. His last sight of his aunt was of her skirts moving like a dust storm, her back turned to them. Her footfalls ricocheted off Salvatore's murmured commentary about *cosi di fimmini*, the last of these denouncing Rosaria's entire family: "'Sorry is the house where the distaff commands the sword.'" With this, he put his cap on his head, called to Paolo, and began walking.

They passed *Sant'Agata's* northern wall and began trudging towards a brown speck on the horizon. This, his grandfather informed him, was where they were headed. Although his view was blurred by the dust on the landscape, Paolo decided, from what he could see, that the baron's estate resembled any other farmstead in Sicily. No moats or minarets were evident.

Nonetheless, Paolo was intrigued by the thought of meeting the baron. He had some questions about the man, and he wasn't going to let his grandfather's bad mood get in the way of his curiosity: "When you were talking about the baron, grandfather, what did you mean when you said, 'He was with us?'"

His grandfather, still fuming over Rosaria's insolence, flailed his arms with impatience. "You with your questions!!" He shook a forefinger in Paolo's face, in exact imitation of Giuseppe's gesture the day before. "I could fall into a mine, and you'd throw me a question instead of a rope."

Paolo waited to repeat the inquiry. When he asked again, the sun had climbed into the sky's highest reaches, throwing its harvest of heat and rays onto their heads.

"I suppose there's no reason you shouldn't know," Salvatore replied.

Then it came out: How Salvatore and his brothers had joined up with Garibaldi 30 years before to drive out the Spanish. About the bloodshed and fallen banners and the final preeminence of the Italian flag, flying unfettered and free, on a mountain of the dead. How Paolo and Giuseppe and Salvatore thought they would live just as unencumbered, only to find they were no better off: The hats would not part with their land, nor was anybody going to make them share with the peasants.

"There was no liberty. We were rounded up like cattle when we tried to demand our rights," his grandfather told him. "The baron, our leader, crawled back to that villa of his. He wasn't going to give up anything he didn't have to. And we had no more than we did at the beginning of the revolt.

"And that, Paolo, is why your *Zio* Giuseppe is right." Salvatore seemed surprised at his own concession: "You should never trust a hat."

But Salvatore's story made a larger impact on Paolo than this.

When they reached their destination, Paolo saw that the wrought iron gate of the baron's villa was brown and cracked, like the soil around it. Salvatore swung the gate open, brushed his fingers on the coat of arms on the gate's upper reaches. It was difficult to make out, but Paolo thought he recognized the image of a warthog on the device, a sickle and scythe at its feet.

As Salvatore let the gate clang shut, Paolo set his sights on the baron's house: a brownish, red-roofed building flanked by wings. No more impressive up close, Paolo mused, than miles away.

While his grandfather rapped on the door of the house, Paolo looked around them. The drive encircling the villa had been planted with plane trees, their leaves yellow and drooping in the heat. Inside the wall bordering the yard were plants that grew not naturally, Paolo could tell, but by some gardener's hand. This oasis, composed of roses, medlars, lemon trees, and geraniums, was clustered around a fountain that looked like it had been dry for years. Yet, the harvest was as much in evidence here as anywhere else, signified by rakes and cutting tools, bulging sacks, and a solitary donkey harnessed to a wagon loaded with straw.

When the housekeeper opened the door to the villa, Paolo's grandfather curtly signaled for Paolo to join him. The woman took their names and let them in.

The high, smooth walls that seemed to engulf him on entering the baron's villa reminded Paolo of the piazzas of half a dozen small towns he had been to, including Centuripe. He thought it was incredible for one person to have so much space to call his own. Paolo became more impressed still when his wandering eyes came upon the tall windows set into these walls, composed of innumerable panes of glass, spilling the outdoors light indoors with such abundance that it seemed the baron was in possession of his own personal sun. Then there was the grand staircase, curved like a scorpion's tail; the furniture crafted of wood and metal, cloth and leather; the pictures hanging on the walls from every angle.

To one of these paintings Paolo found himself irresistibly drawn. From where he was standing, he thought he saw standard bearers and cannon and a decorated general (Garibaldi, he guessed) on its warped plane. He moved towards the scene like somebody who was under a spell.

The spell was immediately broken when the housekeeper shouted at him: *"Leviti vostre scharpi!"*

Paolo stared at the woman. He could not have heard what he thought he did.

He turned to his grandfather, whose shoes were off, and who was now taking off his stockings. "She wants your shoes, so you don't soil the rug."

"What's a rug?" Paolo asked. His grandfather pointed to the rich floorcovering beneath their feet. Paolo sat on it, took off his shoes and stockings, and placed them by the door.

"Do what I do," Paolo's grandfather instructed him, and Paolo followed Salvatore, trailing the housekeeper across the rug. As his feet sank into its soft woolen fibers, Paolo thought the sensation must be the same as treading the down of newly hatched chicks, and found himself never wanting to leave the rug, much the way he idled in front of the picture. No wonder the baron was so attached to such things, he mused.

The housekeeper whisked them into another room, this one with a long table and a fireplace. After she departed, Paolo was not surprised his grandfather took the opportunity to reprimand him for not taking his shoes off when he was first asked. "You will put a mask on me with your thick head!" Salvatore wailed.

Paolo was overwhelmed, not for the first time, by the injustice of his grandfather's scolding. He hadn't meant any disrespect by not taking off his shoes. So what, if he was a little slow? What harm had been done? He was tired of his grandfather's outbursts, exhausted from work and hunger; sick of rich people stealing from poor ones, and of the sun robbing the soil.

Just then, Paolo heard a step on the stairs. He noticed, at the same time, that his grandfather's posture began to change. Salvatore's head drooped, and his eyes became engrossed with the floor at his feet. He took off his cap and urged Paolo to do the same.

For ten years Paolo had been under Salvatore's jurisprudence. He had been his grandfather's servant, helpmate, companion; had eaten his scraps, laughed at his jokes, did the lowest, dirtiest part of work that was already dirty and low. He'd been a receiving basket for Salvatore's barbed tongue, and a fishnet for his floating criticisms. He had taken a lot from the man, and a mutiny was overdue, yet why he chose that moment to revolt was a question Paolo could never answer. But revolt is what he did.

"We don't have to take off our caps any longer," Paolo replied. "We're equal to the nobility, remember?"

Paolo's grandfather looked at him with something close to horror. This, while the steps came closer.

Paolo tensed for the expected blow.

"Take off your cap now. Take it off now." Remarkably, Paolo saw that his grandfather wasn't angry. His fierce, formidable grandfather was afraid. It was another injustice Paolo would hold the hats responsible for.

"Don't you remember why you fought, grandfather?" When his grandfather shook his head, Paolo continued: "Well, I do. And if I have to, I'll fight for our rights all over again."

Now his grandfather looked beaten. But only for a moment: "I, as your grandfather, command you to take off your cap! I will disown you..."

"No Salvatore! He's right!" These words came from the baron, standing at the bottom of the staircase.

Both Paolo and his grandfather looked in the direction of the voice. Happy to get a look at the man he had wondered about for so long, Paolo was surprised to see how small he was. But spry and alert, too, like his grandfather. With a light complexion, and eyes the color of unripe olives.

"This must be your grandson,"

Paolo, who knew better than to seek his grandfather's guidance on the point, grasped the hand extended to him.

In the meantime, Salvatore made a dodge for Paolo's hat, but the other man caught his arm in mid-air.

"No, Salvatore. Paolo is right," the baron said.

He turned to gaze at Paolo with approval. "I saw you were looking at the picture of Garibaldi in my receiving room. Here's another battle scene you might like." He walked over to a mural beside the table, while Paolo followed, his eyes wide.

"This is *Calatifimi*, where I fought with your grandfather. We threw the Spanish out of Sicily and did our part to unite Italy."

"Is one of those men my grandfather?" Paolo asked in disbelief.

The baron chuckled. "It's an artist's rendering, but, yes, one of those men could be your grandfather, and your great uncles, too. We gave them a run for their money, didn't we, Salvatore?" Paolo's grandfather, more relaxed on the other side of the table, nodded.

"You're correct to stand up for yourself, Paolo. Your grandfather stops you only because times are hard, and he's afraid to lose the little he has. It's a common human failing." He threw Salvatore a meaningful look.

Spoken like a sage, Paolo pondered, yet with the conspiratorial air of a cousin. Paolo decided he liked the man.

Nonetheless, there was an accounting in order: "Why do you keep the land from the peasants?" he asked. Paolo heard his grandfather groan from across the room.

The baron nodded his head. "Some of the estates were annexed. My family lost their land near *Marsala*." He pointed to one of the maps on the wall.

"But you know, too much change isn't good." By now Paolo was too charmed by the man to disagree, too innocent to see he was being led away from the subject. "Why don't we talk about it over some coffee?"

"Coffee?" asked Paolo. "What's that?"

"You don't know what coffee is? What do you drink for breakfast?"

"*Vino*."

"Oh," The baron laughed. "Of course!"

Salvatore settled his cap on his head. He grasped the bridle of the donkey, the same one that had been attached to the cart he had seen in the yard on approaching the baron's house. When they put his son in the ground, the baron had promised him anything that was in his power to give. Well, the baron had come through. The donkey was laden with wheat that would fetch a high price no matter where it was sold, and with cheese, olives, chickens ready for slaughter. Once clear of the baron's gate, this time opened for them by one of the baron's men, Salvatore sighed with relief.

Things had turned out okay. No thanks to that grandson of his. The baron spent most of their visit talking to Paolo about the history of 30 years ago, while Salvatore sweated in suspense over whether they would eat tomorrow.

Strange world, Salvatore couldn't help thinking, when a man gives decades of service only to be ignored in front of his grandson. When a man doffs his hat to the local nobility and is told to put it back on his head. They fought for their rights, yes, but respect was a different matter.

But things had turned out alright. Despite his grandson's behavior.

What a strange place Sicily was getting to be. For him and his grandson to have coffee and cakes with the baron and hear him invite Salvatore to the estate to work, year-round, on very favorable terms. Not only that, but to insist on sending Paolo to school to learn about numbers. Learning about accounts could really help a man who works the soil…could help anyone.

It was a strange world, when a peasant could get these things from a baron. How he would explain this turn of events to everyone, especially the part about Paolo's behavior, he couldn't say.

The thing his grandson needed to learn was patience. A man reaps what he sows. The unripe fig is best left on the tree. He would teach Paolo, one way or another, even if he had to beat it into him. Eventually he would learn.

He gave the donkey a tug, then patted a leg straddling one side of the beast.

His grandson, seated on the bent back of the donkey, smiled down at him.

THE HAT

The fishwives and women vendors, selling bread or pretzels on the sidewalks, seemed to flash their eyes at Vita like cleavers. With the malevolence, but not the stealth, of assassins, they exchanged looks as she passed with whichever male relative was chaperoning her that day. It was as though they were saying: "What have we here??" often followed by a word or phrase in a dialect Vita had never heard and swore she'd never learn. Even with her protector—brother, uncle, or cousin—it was a purgatory to step among such women on the street.

The men were kinder. Sometimes they called her *Donna*, or even addressed her with the honorific *Vossia*. Even more gratifying, when Vita and her companion reached their destination, the males inside would sweep off their hats to her. This was pleasant, but next would come the ordeal of ordering the veal or pot roast from the butcher who may or may not be able to follow her speech dialect. And the challenge of departing from the bread shop with a single loaf, rather than the three or four the baker usually tried to cram into her bag.

The trolley was her savior. For a nickel, the dense crowds that packed Mulberry Street could be avoided. Vita and her chaperone would sit and survey with their eyes the working men and women of lower Manhattan. Small wonder, she reflected at these times, that she preferred her brother's apartment to rubbing shoulders with such a motley crowd.

Still, her immersion in the urban panorama could not be avoided. Soon after her arrival in New York, her brother Carlo made it clear she would earn her bread. Not that she wasn't used to the sort of busyness permitted to her station and gender in Italy. But there it had been different. For one thing, her father had a certain amount of prestige in her small town. For another thing, no matter where she went in *Sant'Agata*, she was greeted by people she had known and who had nurtured her, in their way, since her limbs had been wrapped in swaddling clothes.

Here, on this street holding ten times the population of her entire native village, she could wander all day and not see the same face twice. And the faces she saw—hard as granite—did not encourage familiarity. Yet, until a marriageable man came along, Vita would reconcile herself to her life's new tableau.

This isn't to say she didn't cling to the bits of her former life that remained. She read the letters from her mother with the same ardor with which she prayed for a husband. She caressed the Sicilian lemons and oranges sold at the markets as though they were the children yet to be coaxed from her womb. And before leaving her brother's apartment, she never failed to attach a little black hat to the top of her dark, glossy hair. Hair streaked with plum and poppy, the way her native landscape smoldered with these hues when the sun rose and set.

Vita had been chided by her cousins and mother at home for wearing the hat. They said that kind of ornamentation was for the wife of a *Don*, and not for an artisan's daughter. Here, it was no different. The midwife across the hall clucked the first time she saw it, and the fishwives and bread vendors laughed when it became clear Vita was just another neighborhood woman (not an uptown visitor) who had the odd notion that a hat was every day attire in her new home.

"That one will come to no good," and "What a sow," they murmured to one another. These things she understood.

When Vita learned Carlo wanted to marry her to the man in the apartment below his own, she nearly choked on her dinner. "That little rat? You want him for a brother-in-law?" she asked.

It was less that he was little and more that she stood higher than most of the women, and many of the men, she knew. The man was known for the stink in his apartment, though. And the children in the building called him "Mouse Eyes" because his eyes looked small and mean.

Carlo placed his hands before his dinner plate on the table. It seemed to Vita that he had trouble meeting her gaze. "There's something you should know. You're being talked about in letters from home since you came to New York," he said.

"Oh?"

"There are people who would say you are not worthy of this man you think so little of."

Vita picked up the cutlet from her plate and threw it across the table. It hit the wall behind Carlo and fell to the floor. Then she departed from the table to go to bed.

They said he ate the ground in big bites, for Orlando had a burning drive to succeed. Yet, while he walked to his midtown construction site in these early morning hours, people from every layer of society—confidence men and salesmen, padrone and professors, bootblacks, doctors, and politicians—greeted him with ease. Native-born Americans and immigrants alike saw *ttechiccenza* (take a chance)—the tendency to seize and make the most of any opportunity that came along—in his robust frame and sculpted face, and he did well in any endeavor his adventurous spirit took on. Even so, those who knew him said Orlando never acted above himself.

The matrons, wives of his brothers and cousins and neighbors, loved his mild, sympathetic manner. His co-workers said, 'One could drink him in a glass of water', because he was known to be good and honest. But he was never too good or too honest. That would not have set well with his bosses at the construction site, known, on occasion, to deliver more sand than was prudent for being poured into his cement mixer.

The old men called him "The Sage," for once he intervened in a dispute between two gangs, preventing them from destroying the relative peace in the surrounding blocks. Orlando never said how he did it, but it was no little help, in the days following, that he offered jobs on his own construction crew to many of the men involved.

All that Carlo knew about Orlando was he was well-liked and steadily employed. Carlo had just received a letter from his wife saying she would make another attempt to join him in New York. He had no appetite for living with both a wife and a sister.

Vita had to be married. Orlando seemed as good a choice as any.

Orlando happened to see Vita as he was entering the building where she and Carlo lived. Not that he knew the woman, surrounded at the time by neighborhood matrons, was Vita. He had come to talk to Carlo about his sister, who needed a husband. As he came to where the women crowded together like thunderheads, it became clear to Orlando that the meeting he rushed to attend put him in a position to help a young woman who was in trouble.

He was pretty sure one of the matrons had dumped a pot close to Vita's hems. As Vita swerved to avoid this muck on the street, she nearly fell on a housewife juggling a mop and broom.

"*Idiota!*" the housewife said.

"A good woman shouldn't have to step around this garbage," said another matron.

Orlando stepped between Vita and her assailants. Sweeping his arm close, he opened a space and indicated, with a swift nod, that she should make her escape. Without a word, Vita turned back to the building from which she had come.

Furious, the feminine mob exchanged words with Orlando, attracting onlookers at street-level and at the windows concealed by the laundry hanging overhead. The yelling match ended only when Orlando cried "*basta!*" in a baritone that would have been applauded in an opera house. At this, the women retreated, dropping insults behind them.

Orlando was still perturbed by these events when he knocked on the door to Carlo's second floor apartment. A new round of astonishment swept over him when he saw the strain and exhaustion coloring Carlo's face as the door opened. Hearing the unmistakable sobs of a woman on walking in, Orlando had an uncomfortable feeling.

"That was…?" Orlando began.

Carlo paused, and then concurred with Orlando's unfinished question: "Yes. That was my sister in the street.

"I don't know why they don't like her." He pulled out a handkerchief to blot his forehead. "Every day when I come home, she's in tears. If I believed in that kind of thing, I'd say she was touched by the Evil Eye. It's..." he searched for the right word. "It's..."

"It's the hat," said Orlando, surprising himself. So much, he took a moment to picture the young, pretty woman. Yes, she wore a hat. Of this, he was sure.

"What hat??" Carlo demanded.

It would not have been in character for Carlo to pay attention to the way his sister or any other woman adorned herself. What with working to support his wife and son (who were presently in Sicily), recruiting for his union, and toiling to further his other radical causes, Carlo saw his sister little and spoke with her less. Only lately had it occurred to him that Vita wasn't adjusting to her new home. He was sure the remedy for this was marriage.

Yet, while Carlo had little else in common with the capitalists of the land, he did, along with every man he knew, don a hat before leaving for work in the morning. It was a behavior that didn't seem the least bit strange to him. And at that very moment Carlo seemed to recall Vita was wearing one before leaving on her aborted errand.

"What about it?" Carlo asked.

"None of the women around here wears one. Is your father a *Don*? A duke, a baron?"

"Of course not. We call him a harness maker, but he makes all kinds of leather accessories. I'm with the people..."

Orlando interrupted what could turn into one of Carlo's Labor speeches.

"Well then, she is putting on airs. I don't know how it is in *Sant'Agata*, but the women around here don't like a person to act above themselves. If you were a company owner, it might be alright. But even then, she'd be entitled to the hat only if she were married to one," said Orlando. He twisted his own cap in his hands as he spoke.

Carlo assumed a thoughtful expression. Since her arrival Vita had been exactly as he had always known her to be. Her graceful figure, quiet and dignified, her observant eyes that took in everything but gave back nothing—all were like emblems of home for him. Except for the shocking stories coming from the other side of the Atlantic, he would change nothing. Her very immutability—the fact that she remained as she had been before he left Italy, was reassuring to Carlo. For much had changed in recent years, but Vita had not.

Yet, here was someone saying she needed to be different.

"Well…with or without the hat, she's got to marry," replied Carlo, still thoughtful. "Maybe she needs to change."

Orlando nodded.

"We can work on that. But she is lovely! She can cook and clean…will you court her?"

Now Orlando shook his head. "No."

"No??" Carlo was dumbstruck. Clearly, his sister was not perfect. Still, he remembered how the young men in the village had followed her—most times with their eyes, sometimes with their feet following suit. There was no doubt Orlando was a solid man, but his background was far from illustrious. In Sicily his family often made do for their daily bread with a few greens and the water from the *Ricotta* cooked by a sympathetic landowner.

And Carlo couldn't help but find his idealism being replaced by pride in his own, more fortunate pedigree.

What gives this vagabond the nerve to refuse my sister? Carlo knew better than to voice these thoughts, but the sentiments showed on his face.

Orlando plopped on his cap and turned to go. "*Mi scusi, Signore*. Your sister is nice, I'm sure. But she's not for me."

"Okay. Okay." Carlo used this Americanism with ease. "But don't forget about the Labor meeting on Thursday." He and Orlando discussed the details as they walked out of the apartment and to the stairs.

Two things changed Orlando's mind about marrying Vita. First, his mother in Sicily became sick with malaria. The medicine and doctor visits she required made it necessary for him to find a way to supplement the money he had been sending home since coming to America. When Carlo put out there was a good dowry in it for anyone willing to marry Vita, Orlando began to recast his thoughts about the union organizer's sister.

Second, he'd been observing Vita for a period of months. Orlando always attended the labor-raising meetings held by Carlo and his union cohorts. To these, at the combination bank and bar at the intersection of Mulberry and Hester, where the meetings took place, the young woman came along with Carlo. More interested in her needlework than what was being said, she sat quietly in the corner with a few educated women. Like some of these, she had the lofty air of a stone Madonna.

She was beautiful, Orlando had to admit. But there was the hat. Well, leave it to Carlo's sister to think she was better than everyone else, Orlando's brothers told him. For there were many who thought Carlo's idealism—his clean hands and pure heart—were but an opportunity for him to feign superiority over other men. Little did they know Orlando found Carlo's sister attractive because she did think she was superior. But then, he was unusually ambitious for a fellow of his low birth and prospects.

And now he knew the financial benefits of marrying her. While it was a good opportunity, Orlando thought if Vita were as haughty as she seemed, it would take some doing to win her over.

How to start? Orlando smiled. That was easy. She wore what she most wanted right there on her head. The hat was key.

He went to Carlo to talk.

"Now you want to marry my sister. Fine," said Carlo. The dowry—donated by his father in Italy— was undoubtedly behind Orlando's about face.

"I'll tell her you'll be here tomorrow. Is two o'clock alright?"

Orlando nodded. He was suddenly apprehensive. But he resolved the feeling would not overwhelm him.

When Orlando arrived the next day, he could see that Carlo's apartment had been swept and straightened. Two chairs had been removed from the kitchen and put close to the door, and, to make the courtship ritual somewhat private, they were partly surrounded by a wooden screen. Sunlight spilling in the room's tall windows shone through the screen's latticework, nearly consuming the wooden edifice with its rays.

Orlando himself was scrubbed and shaved. A scent of mint clung to his face, and he wore a new borrowed suit. In his arms he carried two gifts for Vita: one of the colorful shawls sold at Saints' festivals in New York and in Italy, and an orange.

Carlo had opened the door and soon introduced Orlando to the woman who would chaperone the proceedings—the midwife from across the hall. After this nicety had been performed, Carlo exited the apartment with a quick good-bye. His departure left Orlando and Vita without a family member in attendance, a breach of etiquette causing Orlando to realize his first meeting with Vita would be nothing like the *canuscenzas* of Sicily. Worse still, the midwife sprang out of her chair to speak with him as soon as Carlo was gone.

"She's a well-straddled mare," the woman whispered, with soggy lips, in Orlando's ear. "It was a soldier from Capua…"

Vita's entrance sped the woman—whose name was Peppina—back into her chair. The midwife went back to her knitting as if no one else was in the room. Orlando began to feel distinctly uncomfortable, and Vita looked none too happy. Yet, with hints of determination in the way she straightened her back and squared her shoulders, the young woman sat down.

For forty minutes neither Orlando nor Vita said a word. No word was said right up until Orlando looked at the borrowed watch hanging from his vest pocket and prepared to leave. Just as he was pulling himself to his feet, the orange, in his lap beneath the shawl, rolled to the floor.

Vita rose from her chair to capture the fruit in her hands.

"This is a blood-orange," she said with clear delight.

"*Si, si, Signorina*," Orlando agreed. "Pietro sells them on my street…"

"We grow these where I come from, in Sant'Agata."

Her sudden interest in the orange brought a luster to the dark irises of Vita's eyes.

"Do you?" Orlando smiled. "I never saw one until I came to New York."

They went on to talk about the fruit sold by the produce vendors in the street, the crops grown in the towns they came from, and how the droughts and varied disasters in Sicily had brought the two of them to America. Orlando was later able to say the meeting had been a success. This, despite almost blatant efforts on the part of Vita's brother and the chaperone to make it otherwise.

"She's a well-straddled mare." Orlando remembered the midwife's statement. Evidently, Vita had a past. That would explain her brother's interest in having a humble man court her, her sudden arrival in New York, the astounding dowry offered with her hand.

He should not, he knew, attach himself to such a worn cane. He believed the traditional wisdom that any mortal sin committed by a man was venial, while any venial sin by a woman was mortal. Yet, Orlando decided to stay the course. He remembered again how it had been like blasting stone to penetrate the woman's initial shyness. How the splendor of her smile—when a smile finally came to her face—seemed almost to blind him.

Perhaps because he knew the first visit had not ended in disaster, Carlo stayed in the apartment when Orlando visited again. This time, some of Carlo and Vita's relatives were in attendance, as was Orlando's brother, Francesco. Among the gifts Orlando brought to give to Vita on this day were shoes—shimmering with satin and rhinestones, far too expensive for his purse—and a statue of the Virgin Mary.

He had the idea the shoes could suggest wealth and position, hoping to reassure Vita she would not be yoked to a simple construction foreman for long. He bought the Madonna out of respect for the religious sentiments he had been told she had, though he himself was not a religious man. He would not tell her these things in words, because he wasn't sure how. He hoped, rather, that these sentiments would be imparted by his gifts, perhaps with the aid of the heavenly intercession on which she relied.

As he watched her eyes and hands explore the statue's smooth porcelain contours and lovely painted-on face, Orlando knew the Virgin did, indeed, hold special significance for Vita. Still, when her caresses and comments on the statue's beauty came to an end, the light in her eyes seemed to dim, and her smile waned. And Orlando wondered if his reason for giving her the statue had been misunderstood. If the image of the chaste Holy Mother perhaps made her ashamed of her own, less virginal, state.

He leaned in closely to capture her attention as she sat stiffly, her eyes cast down, her hands folded in her lap. The rest of the guests were on the other side of the room.

"The priests say the Holy Mother is the most beautiful woman in the world, untouched for eternity. I wonder if they know that most of us are not so perfect. My own mother,

Signorina, did not marry my father. Yet I could not love her more if she was the Mother of God."

Vita looked up, slowly. When she caught his eyes with her own, he could see she understood what he was telling her. And he saw those tongues of light restored to her eyes, like sun rays capturing ripples on water.

Satisfied he had won Vita's heart, Orlando warmed to Carlo's suggestion that they go into the hallway 'to smoke'—his way of saying they should talk about the dowry. Orlando begged Vita's leave, while Carlo drifted to the back of the flat to find his cigarettes.

The door to the hallway had remained open throughout Orlando's visit, with neighbors stopping in now and then. Ostensibly they came to say hello, but Orlando guessed the news that Vita was getting engaged had traveled the building. They wanted to see what kind of catch the reluctant fisher had netted.

Peppina, as luck would have it, was at this time returning from delivering a baby. The old midwife was an accomplished gossip who knew when the mold grew in every tenement flat on the block. She had the news of Vita's engagement even before she entered the building. Evidently thinking it was her duty to prevent Orlando from yoking himself to such a "well-straddled mare", she wasted no time telling everyone in the room her opinion of the match.

"Dishonor and shame will come to you," she declared, locking her eyes with Orlando's.

Vita broke into tears. "Carlo! Come here!" she called out.

Orlando, while touched by the faith Vita had in her brother's abilities, could think of nothing Carlo could do to remedy the situation. Peppina had cast her black spell on the proceedings, and, allowed to continue, she could effectively eliminate Vita's chances for a marriage on both sides of the Atlantic.

Even now, the onlookers—unsure what had occurred—looked in apprehension and curiosity from Orlando to Vita to Peppina. When Carlo came back into the room with his cigarettes, their gaze shifted to him.

"What's wrong?" Carlo asked. "What's happened here?"

Orlando was at a loss about what to do or say. Aware that one strong word from Peppina could force him to call off the engagement, he was mulling it over when Carlo's characteristic impatience brought the situation to a tipping point.

"Will you tell me, Orlando—once and for all—what is going on here?" he demanded.

Thinking fast, Orlando assumed an earnest look. "*Si, si.* I will tell you. Though you may not like it."

"Oh?" Carlo replied. Orlando saw Carlo take in his sister's crestfallen face.

"It is something I've told no one in this country. But I see it wouldn't be right—as we are to be family—to have secrets between us."

"Oh??" More emphatically.

"Si. I have no wish to bring dishonor to you or your sister. I beg your pardon for keeping it from you, but I know now I should tell you…"

"If you go on like this," said Carlo, "you will make me curse, Orlando! Tell me, already!"

"Alright!" And Orlando warmed to Carlo's impatience, for it added to the suspense he was building.

"I'm not a Sicilian."

"Not a Sicilian?" Carlo looked more dumbstruck than when Orlando told him he wouldn't court Vita.

"I was born across the straits. My mother is from *Messina*." And now Orlando had the same look of expectant dread, though his was contrived, that had been on Vita's face when Peppina denounced their engagement.

Once more, the onlookers looked from Vita, to Orlando, and to Carlo. Only Peppina's interest had evaporated. For his part, Carlo continued to look perplexed, and his eyes held a shade of doubt, as though he was relatively sure the place where Orlando was born was not what the fuss was about.

Now Peppina revealed the reason for her indifference. "Not a Sicilian? Why then, you're not a Christian. You two are perfect for each other." And she retreated to her apartment.

The suspicion in Carlo's eyes cleared up. "Not a Sicilian?" he asked whimsically. "Well, this is a surprise. But I won't turn you away for that. Vita wouldn't forgive me." And he led Orlando out of the building for their talk.

"'He who uses a hat, adores the devil.'" This was the response of Orlando's brother, Benedetto, when he learned that a date had been assigned to the marriage between Orlando and Vita.

"But she's a nice girl, despite the hat..." Orlando replied.

"A nice girl? Tell me, Orlando, what do you know about this woman?" And he tendered one of the countless Sicilian proverbs about marriage: "'Women and bulls from your own town only.' That's what mother used to say! And she was right!"

"That may have held true in Sicily, Benedetto, but things are different here. I couldn't find a woman from our town if I tried to. I've told you: I met her, and I like her."

"Is it the woman, or her dowry that's right for you?" And to the violent shaking of Orlando's head: "You seem to forget: 'A wife with a large dowry unhorses her husband.'"

"And you, Benedetto, forget: 'the dowry hides the defects of the bride,'" said Orlando, demonstrating he had proverbs of his own to offer.

"Oh, so you admit…"

Orlando didn't let him finish. "I admit," he said, pounding the table for emphasis, "that 'a good wife is the primary wealth of the house.' Vita has all the makings of a good wife, with or without the dowry. And I intend to marry her."

"She's a devil. And it's not only me who thinks so! If you marry "The Hat", my wife will never visit you! And you can forget I'm your brother!"

Orlando drew back to look at Benedetto. He knew there was nothing he could do or say to pacify his brother in such a state.

"Okay. If I marry "The Hat" you'll no longer be my brother," Orlando agreed. "Fine. Just promise me one thing."

"What's that?" Benedetto asked.

"That you'll come to the wedding."

"I just finished telling you…"

"I know", Orlando countered. "I know what you said. I'll take care of it. Now promise."

Benedetto sighed: "Fine." But Orlando knew he said it only to end the discussion. Whether he and his wife would attend the wedding was anyone's guess.

Orlando was not disappointed to learn the wedding was postponed until Carlo's wife, Nora, made the crossing from Italy. The delay worked well with his plans. Guessing it would take a herculean effort to separate Vita from her hat, Orlando welcomed having an extra four weeks to make it happen. He was soon to learn four weeks was not nearly enough time.

Orlando first tried to dissuade Vita from wearing her hat by poking fun at the women's hats displayed in the shops and department stores he and Vita passed on their evening strolls together. She would surely not wear a garment her fiancée found ridiculous. But Vita was always wearing that infernal hat of hers next time he came calling! Thinking to enlist Carlo's help, Orlando told his future brother-in-law that Vita's continued use of the hat would not be looked on kindly by her in-laws. Carlo said he'd do what he could, but after a week or two, his efforts had come to nothing.

Orlando's final attempt took a comedic turn when, as they watched a marionette show one day in the park, he departed from Vita's side to retrieve a fishing reel secreted behind the puppeteer's stage and used it to dispatch the hat off her head. The onlookers thought it was part of the act, and Vita did too.

Ironically, even as he tried to get her to stop wearing it, Orlando was losing his own objections to the hat. No longer did he fear or was he offended by what the hat represented to Vita or anyone else. Indeed, he wanted her to keep it. Not only because in due time he knew she would be entitled to it as his wife. Nor because he liked to be with a woman who dressed in style.

He supposed it was because he was, as they said in Sicily, "enchained" to his betrothed. He was passionate about his intended and their future together. So much, he could overlook a pretension he found quite silly, because it made her happy.

These were feelings he would never be able to share with Benedetto. To be at the behest of a woman would make him a laughing stock in his older brother's eyes. And the pull of these conflicting loyalties, for Benedetto on the one hand, and Vita on the other, made him see he might have to choose. But if it came to that, he knew what his choice would be.

As the wife of a Labor activist, Nora was no less dedicated to the cause than her husband was. Resolved to enlist her *paisanas* to join a women's auxiliary for the same union Carlo recruited for, she took it upon herself to learn her women neighbors' attitudes towards Labor soon after arriving in New York.

Due to the woman's unrivaled reputation as gossip, snoop, and purveyor of (usually bad) news, her mission took Nora straight to Peppina's door. Not surprisingly, the midwife talked about more than just Labor. She was only too happy to share the revelation—astonishing to Nora—that Orlando's family threatened to disown him if he married "The Hat", the nickname given Vita by the faction that took offense at the headpiece she insisted on wearing in public.

This is how it fell on her sister-in-law, Nora, to tell Vita about the disdain her neighbors and acquaintances had for what she saw as a harmless decoration for her head.

Vita was standing before the mirror in the parlor, matching jewelry to her wedding dress, when Nora came through the door with the unhappy news. Nora had debated with herself mightily on the way home whether to share the horrid tale with Vita, but decided in the end it was a betrayal not to. She would tell her young sister-in-law, with as much gentleness as possible, that her future in-laws were arrayed against her, and, most especially, the reason they had for disliking her.

Learning it all for the first time, Vita's face became flushed with anger and embarrassment, and she began to cry. With the help of the handkerchief she always kept in her corset, Nora removed the tears on Vita's cheeks with a kindly and experienced hand. When the young women's crying was spent, the two of them had a long, quiet talk.

They were still talking when Carlo arrived home. Aware that something extraordinary had occurred, Carlo bided his time to hear about it from his wife. Then he sat down to read his newspaper.

Despite predictions it would never happen, the wedding was held on a fine day in April. Many members of both families, even Benedetto and his wife, were in attendance. The bride was lovely in a borrowed red taffeta gown, her dark hair upswept and accented by a white rose pinned to one side. Orlando looked as austere and formal as Vita had ever seen him, wearing a new dark-blue suit, a borrowed handkerchief, and the same gold watch he wore for their courtship tucked in his pocket.

There was a distinct hush inside the church after the marriage contract had been signed. Vita couldn't be sure if it was the end or just the beginning of hostilities between the factions that were assembled—those for and against "The Hat." Little did either side understand, as Vita did, that her hat no longer had the power to derail the future that she and Orlando had planned together.

This turn of events would be evident only later. First the rites of a Sicilian wedding celebration would take place. For this, the front room of Nora and Carlo's apartment was as crowded as it had ever been, with chairs donated from every neighbor on the floor pushed up against the wall. As the guests streamed in, each made their presence known to the bride and groom before placing a wedding gift on a nearby table. Presently everyone was seated, and Vita and Nora served them sweets, wine, and liqueurs.

Not long after a small dinner had been served, Orlando's distant cousins serenaded Vita, with one brother playing a mandolin, the other singing love songs. When the evening shadows began to fall, another guest played the bagpipes while a few adventurous couples pushed back the table to dance. This merry episode did not last for long, however, for soon banging could be heard coming from the apartment below, and the dancing and bagpipe music were brought to a close.

The noisy objection from the downstairs neighbor was a clear signal the celebration had to end. The guests departed their chairs and, with animated chatter, began forming a line to the table where the wedding gifts had been placed. One-by-one they picked up their offerings—gifts that were as varied as the means of the guests who gave them—and handed them over to Vita and Orlando.

Finally, only two boxes remained.

"What's this?" Benedetto demanded, on seeing the gifts that lacked a claimant. He had been haunting the edges of the reception, casting his eyes everywhere to search for clues whether or not Vita and Orlando's union would last. He, personally, had not brought a gift, for he thought it was enough he was attending, although he saw no evidence that Vita had stopped wearing her hat, as had been promised.

"One of the boxes is my present to Vita," Orlando explained.

"The other is my gift to Orlando," said Vita.

"Well, open them," Benedetto said. He pushed his chair forward to sit near the couple, the better to see how they reacted to the gifts they gave each other.

Vita was the first to open her gift. She unwrapped a large box that bore the slogan and markings of one of the large uptown department stores. With an air of reverence, she put the contents of this box on the table.

It was a lady's silk dark blue hat.

Vita was astonished.

After hearing what Nora had said about her in-laws' hatred for the hat she already wore, she had to wonder why Orlando would publicly defy his family by giving her another one. Not surprisingly, the wedding guests displayed an air of puzzlement, too.

Benedetto rose to his feet in shock and anger: "Is this how you 'take care' of making sure your wife no longer wears the hat? By adding to her collection?"

"Benedetto…" said Orlando, in his most reasonable tone. "I wanted to talk to you, but there wasn't time. So, I'll tell you now: I won't let a hat come between me and Vita."

"But you let it come between you and your family!"

"I won't ask Vita to be something she isn't."

"What nonsense!!" Benedetto said in disbelief. "It may be late for you to see, but Vita didn't only marry a man, she married a family, too."

Orlando responded with equal surprise: "Then why didn't *you* say 'I do'"?

The debate touched a chord with the guests, who, while disturbed to see hard words exchanged on what should be a happy occasion, were plainly interested in what was being said. Some showed partiality—by a raised eyebrow or brief nod—for one or the other brother's point of view.

Presently, some of them opened the debate with each other. Vita and Nora looked in horror as wives shook fingers at husbands, and families revisited feuds with in-laws. Gradually, a low, angry buzz overtook the room.

Vita stepped between the brothers.

"Open my gift, Orlando," she urged.

Orlando stepped away from Benedetto to unwrap the one gift that remained. The box contained Vita's black hat—the one that had caused such controversy due to her insistence on wearing it. She had wrapped it in a package tied with a beautiful bow.

"I give you a hat and now you're giving your hat to me? What is this?" Orlando asked.

"Vita's trying to tell you something," Nora suggested, against Carlo's protests.

"Trying to tell us all that she is a stubborn mule," Benedetto added.

"I don't need the hat anymore," said Vita. The guests disengaged from their own talk to listen.

"Don't give up the hat for me…" said Orlando.

"But I will give it up…"

Orlando reluctantly nodded. "Mark my words," he said. "One day you will wear the hat because you'll be entitled to it."

"I will put it on then. In the meantime, I'll follow your lead in this. Not because anyone says I have to." Benedetto failed to realize the remark was meant for him. "But because I want to."

There was, by now, a collective hush in the room.

The honey of Vita and Orlando's shared declaration of love had changed the mood of the gathering. The wedding guests, touched to the core to have witnessed this first drama in the married lives of the couple, clapped with approval. Rarely did one see so much emotion have such perfect resolution, and there were murmurs about the "True Sicilian Love" of Vita and Orlando. The young girls, in particular, took out their handkerchiefs to dab the tears pooling in their eyes. And if it all seemed a bit too dramatic for everyday life and simple people, it was, after all, a wedding celebration, with a good many attendees inebriated by wine, as well as sentiment.

This emotional outpouring was lost on Benedetto, though he was happy to hear Vita was giving up wearing her hat. Still, he wanted to be sure she didn't go back to wearing one.

"Somebody needs to do something with these hats," he said loudly, pointing to the gift table.

The wedding singer came forward. "My wife's birthday is next week. I can take them off your hands," he said.

And then, to the frown creasing Benedetto's forehead, as he pictured his own wife ending up the pariah that Vita had been: "Or, I can take them to the thrift store. Who needs a hat, anyway?"

THE WITCH ON BLEECKER STREET

The child was wailing again.

Looking out the window, *Zia* Maria stood on her kitchen table, just barely able to see the patch of sparse grass where three tenements converged. Here is where the little girl sat crying on the street curb, head bent dolefully. Behind her, girls danced with glee around an imaginary mulberry bush.

Zia Maria made the sign of the cross, touching fingers to her forehead, breast, and shoulders, one at a time, while asking God to grant his mercy on the unhappy child before her. She sighed, causing her low, heavy bosom to dance across the top of her stomach.

How she would like to help *la mischina* play with the other children without a care. For a reason known to the Almighty only, it was not God's will. God's ways were mysterious. But she, at least, had some recourse.

Now where was that bottle of Oil of Laurel? It was a costly ingredient for her magic potions, but well worth the price, for it was the foundation for a litany of cures that put the Savior's miracles to shame. Oil of Laurel was especially good for soothing arthritis, rheumatism and gout, these days the most common ailments bringing clients to her door. For the storied generation that came from across the sea—her generation—was aging. The damp and drafts of the cold-water flats where they lived were perfect for inflaming old limbs. Her elderly neighbors came to her, leaning on their grown-up children, or she to them, and she applied ointment and wrapped their aching legs or arms in hot wool.

Like all Sicilian healers, *Zia* Maria believed there was a treatment for every illness. Chief among them were hundreds, even thousands, of herbal remedies, "as many herbs as there are diseases." Moreover, like her Sicilian brethren, *Zia* Maria knew while the ideal was to treat a sickness at its onset, early intervention did not always work. And when efforts over years bore no fruit, the long-standing condition, like a stealthy serpent, was sure to bring death to the sufferer.

She rifled through the jars and bottles, canisters, flour bags, vials, and boxes piled on the shelves in her kitchen. In addition to these, she had a wealth of materials she had scavenged: candle stubs and empty spools; tongue depressors; rags; cigar boxes; campaign pins; glass; cotton, wool, and linen cloth; rope; bottle caps; string; rubber; pipe-cleaners; and wire. The odds and ends came in handy. But most especially, they gave *Zia* Maria the feeling she was prepared for anything. Never did she believe this more than when a neighbor came to ask for a bit of rubber or string. They knew *Zia* Maria had everything they could need!

Ah! The Oil of Laurel, at last! She cupped the small bottle in her hands, backing from the shelves just at the moment the little girl's cries hit a crescendo. *Zia* Maria shook her head. She had a mind to put a hex on the whole lot of them, except little Lina. God knew she had more than enough reason.

For several months now, she had been witnessing this little girl, four, maybe five years-old, being treated like an outsider, at best, or at worst an animal escaped from the zoo, by the other children. *Zia* Maria thought lately Lina had lost hope the cruelty she suffered was going to end, hence her crying every day for the last two weeks. There could be no mystery what repulsed the girl's peers. Lina had been born with a long dark smudge, a birthmark to some, a mole, to others, on the side of her face. A mark smothering her cheek like none that *Zia* Maria had ever seen.

Zia Maria descended to her knees to slide to the floor—not an easy maneuver for somebody her age—only to find she couldn't uncurl her legs. After some pouting, she told herself it was no matter. The dilemma of being stuck on her knees was the Almighty's reminder for her to pray for little Lina and anyone who came to her for a cure.

Closing her eyes, *Zia* Maria began reciting the Rosary, caressing the beads at her waist. Her eyes misty as she came to the Sorrowful Mysteries, she thought it not entirely by chance that Lina's crying hit a peak again. It was a sign. She needed to help that little one.

The old woman sighed once more. It wasn't like she didn't have enough to do, what with her regular clients and new cases of measles and scarlet fever in the building. Even so, the girl could not be overlooked. *Zia* Maria shook her scraggly white hair, and tears filled her clear blue eyes to slide down her stretched and sagging skin. If God wanted so much, why did he not give her a new helper? Once her daughter had filled this role, but with the birth of Angela's sixth child, *Zia* Maria, recalling her own trials with a family of eight, decided to manage on her own.

Of course, her husband, Rosario, called *Cori Rranni* for his big heart, had helped when he could. *Zia* Maria's eyes became pensive as her thoughts turned to him. Dead for ten years now, Rosario had been born to the role of martyr. Tirelessly he had supported the parents and siblings he left behind in Sicily, regardless of how she pleaded with him to let his family stand on their own. He was like that—helping anyone in their season of sickness and old age. The priests applauded him, his co-workers call him *valenti* (worthy) and *burduni* (stupid), in turns, while she, his wife, had despaired of ever having a husband who put his wife and children first.

With his death, she felt shame for the contempt—natural enough when a man takes bread from his children—she had for *Cori Rranni* while he lived. Her own heart had grown big for his sake, befriending those abandoned by friends and family, using her natural healing and magic powers to help and defend the downtrodden.

Finished praying, *Zia* Maria made the sign of the cross. Dangling her bare legs over the side of the table, she slid to the cold tiles below. Once the spare little woman with the large breasts hit the floor, she looked around in surprise. What was she doing there? Then she remembered…ah… she had been looking for her Oil of Laurel. It was here, in her hand. Now she could heat the water for the wool for her morning clients to wrap their aching limbs in.

Fetching her large pot, she remembered a proverb spoken often by her mother: "Promises to Saints and children must be kept always." While she had not promised anything to Lina personally, it was no coincidence she could see the child's sufferings. She would, she decided, cast a spell of protection for her. Yes, and hang a saint's image round Lina's neck, getting some of the girl's hair for the spell at that time. It was only right. Two works of mercy, like stepping stones, leading her to Rosario in Paradise.

Ann Becker could just barely follow Dr. Lawrence's meandering explanation. To hide her confusion, she briefly glanced out the office's third-story window, not daring to remove her eyes from the Lower Manhattan map on the easel before them for more than those few seconds.

"Are you listening, Miss Becker?"

Ann put a neutral expression on her face before turning to face Dr. Lawrence. She could not afford to alienate the Director of the Division of Disease Prevention at the New York City Board of Health. Still, she found his need to have her absolute attention draining.

"Yes, Doctor, I have been."

"Alright, what did I say?" Ann looked at him blankly. Lawrence smirked, his eyes like a sharpshooter who just hit the bull's eye at a kiddy arcade.

"Miss Becker, do you know how many people are under jurisdiction of the Division of Disease Prevention?"

"No, I don't." she admitted.

"More than the population of Connecticut." Ann was from that state's city of Hartford.

"You are aware that Manhattan is an incessant fever den?"

"I can't say that. I know the population density…"

133

"Do you know how this city managed to cut tuberculosis deaths in half between 1900 and 1920?" asked Lawrence, ignoring her. "Not by plastering broadsides saying 'Don't drink the milk' on the walls. It took a concerted, multi-faceted, strategic effort. We went to homes, inspected food and milk supplies, opened clinics and a sanitorium. We taught people who were already infected how to live with the disease."

"Nobody holds a candle to the New York Board of Health! That what you want me to say?" Ann asked, testily.

"Of course not. But don't fight me, either."

"I'm not. I just wonder if these measures are extreme for an epidemic that hasn't hit."

Dr. Lawrence turned again to the map. "Five cases of typhoid fever last month, 9 this month."

"Yes, 5 last month, 9 this month. But even you said it was a normal number of cases for this time of the year."

"And...", Dr. Lawrence drew out the word, "a steamship from Germany had 2 cases onboard last month, with as many as 50 passengers observed in the marine hospital for having contact with the sufferers."

"None sick," Anne shot back.

"Not yet," Lawrence observed. "But there could be carriers. In which case our 14 cases can double overnight."

Ann nodded. It was almost like trying to predict when a serial murderer would strike next. The Board of Health was as perpetually vigilant as any government agency or police department charged with protecting the public. The criminal was disease, the accomplice the poor sanitary and hygienic conditions where it thrived.

And the institution's efforts to reduce the grip of both on the lives and fortunes of New Yorkers had paid. Cases and deaths from influenza, diphtheria, smallpox, yellow fever, malaria, and typhus had nose-dived in the decades since the Board of Health's inception. Even the white plague of tuberculosis, a widespread disease with no known cure or vaccine, was waning. And the last influenza outbreak was strikingly less severe than the previous year's pandemic, due, Lawrence said, to the cooperation of every health professional in the city.

Yet, Disease Prevention could not afford to lose sight of the hotbed of contagion that was the metropolis, where there was always another germ or viral malefactor lurking. This was especially true in the over-crowded tenements of Lower Manhattan. Here, a mix of ethnicities and sensibilities, including Jews, Poles, Irish, Russians, Italians, and other Eastern and Southern Europeans—meant a careful, but firm approach was needed to encourage modern medical and hygienic practices. Most had come to American shores knowing only enough to gain the rudiments of modern living.

"We serve the refuse of Europe," is how Lawrence put it. "They wash up like the garbage released by the steam liners that bring them to our shores. We, the inheritors of the cultural legacies they let fall to rack and ruin, must open their eyes to the way forward. It will take a swift kick (if you will excuse the expression) to turn them around, and it won't come easily—not for us or for them."

Ann arched her brow with a skepticism she doubted Lawrence would ever learn to recognize. "Isn't that harsh? They are people like you and me."

"Are they?" He stared at her the way, she would learn, he looked at people he thought were inferior to him. "You read the papers."

"Well…but…" Here, Ann's insides became tangled up and so did her tongue.

The man was wrong. But he was her boss and influential with the Board of Health. So, her words drifted to nothingness, something that happened often when she spoke to Dr. Lawrence.

Zia Maria had the very good fortune to spy Lina just as she was returning home from shopping in the commercial district on Mulberry Street. Leaning heavily on her wooden cane, her grocery basket nestled in her hip, *Zia* Maria saw the child on the edge of the makeshift playground where several other girls played. She sat quietly, sucking her thumb.

Surveying Lina's lonely state, *Zia* Maria felt a stab of pity. How she would like to put a binding spell on those girls, so they would no longer bother her. Making them like Lina was a different matter, perhaps not hers to meddle with. A simple binding spell, though, would prevent them from being unkind and harassing Lina. Unfortunately, *Zia* Maria had resolved to stop practicing black magic when *Cori Rrani* had died.

It was true a binding spell was supposed to have no affect other than to stop the one who received it from causing harm. This was the reason her sister witches (fewer with each passing year) claimed such spells were not black. But the one warlock she had known insisted a binding spell was black magic. And such a spell could go wrong, making the bewitched person powerless in areas of their lives it was not meant to impact. Determined to meet Rosario in the afterlife, *Zia* Maria decided not to take any chances. A simple spell of protection would have to be enough for Lina.

For this, she needed some personal article belonging to the little girl. Hair would do nicely. In fact, it was the easiest object for the witch wanting to cast a spell to acquire. For this reason, many of *Zia* Maria's age were careful to track their stray hairs and those of their family members.

Lina, of course, was too young for such fears. Still, *Zia* Maria approached her gingerly, mindful her old and gnarled appearance could unsettle such a young and tender shoot.

"Buongiorno bambina." *Zia* Maria said. The little girl took scant notice. "Are you feeling alright, my little one?"

At first Lina continued to suck her thumb and look straight ahead. Soon, however, she seemed to think better of it. Glancing at *Zia* Maria sideways, she creased her forehead whilst giving a little shrug.

"Is your mother at work?"

Her forehead still puckered, Lina said: *"Si."*

"I have something to keep you company." With this, *Zia* Maria slipped a ribbon with a picture of Saint Nicholas, patron saint of children, on the child's neck. Then, quick as Spring, she took a pair of sheers from her pocket and clipped a lock of the child's hair.

Just like that, it was done. She had the hair! *Zia* Maria pressed the golden-brown lock to her lips and slipped it in her pocket. Now she would be able to cast a spell of protection to keep little Lina safe from the other children.

The monthly meeting of Disease Prevention featured a map crisscrossed with colored ink, showing the progress of a diphtheria epidemic.

"Dr. Copeland already sent his statement to the press," Dr. Lawrence informed the assembled health inspectors and educators for the bureau. "Two-thousand seven-hundred seventy-three cases for the city since the year began. We're averaging 60 cases a day. Two-hundred seventy-four deaths, most under the age of 5," he elaborated.

"He wants a plan from us. We need pamphlets, talks, visitations. There's a vaccine for diphtheria, so there shouldn't be an epidemic, in theory. That's where you come in. Contact the schools, churches, movie theatres. Distribute circulars stating the facts: We have an epidemic. People are dying. Here's where you get a Schick Test or inoculation."

"Public clinics go on there," an inspector chimed in.

"And we need posters," suggested a woman inspector.

"I said send out circulars," Lawrence responded.

"They're different. Circulars are circulated. Posters are posted."

Everyone laughed. "Very well, Miss Coyle, you take charge of printed notifications—circulated or posted."

Miss Coyle nodded.

"Get the stats from the press release. We don't need any inconsistencies pressing our credibility at a time like this," Lawrence added. "The public education piece has been fleshed out. We're placing importance on convincing parents to have their children tested with the Schick Test. For those of you who don't know what a Schick Test is, there's the door. For those of you who know the Schick Test, we'll include a list of venues on the printed notifications," he finished.

"For inoculations, too," Miss Coyle said.

"Yes, Miss Coyle! Inoculations, too!!" Lawrence bristled.

With this, Dr. Lawrence's subordinates—Ann and Miss Coyle included—picked up their notebooks and departed.

Zia Maria dropped her grocery bag on the fifth-floor stairway landing. How she wished the building had one of those—what did you call it? A lift or some such thing for taking her up and down, so she wouldn't have to battle her strength and nerves climbing steps. And now…oh *Madre Beddu*…she had the leg cramps…

Leaning against the stair railing, she caught sight of a shadow, the perimeter which just barely touched the hem of her skirt.

"Okay, *Zia* Maria?"

The voice startled her. So much, *Zia* Maria's knees hit the floor. Before she could fall further, the figure attached to the shadow caught her arms by the wrists. A man, tall, handsome, and well-dressed, pulled *Zia* Maria to her feet gently.

"Okay?"

"*Si, si*…you are?"

"You don't know me, *Zia* Maria? I'm Joe Carpaccio's son," he answered in *Zia* Maria's dialect.

Zia Maria threw her arms around her rescuer to embrace him.

"Whooa… easy!" He cautioned.

"Sit here," and he helped *Zia* Maria to lower herself onto the top step.

Gesturing for her to stay put, the man went into a nearby apartment and emerged with a cup of water, the occupant of the apartment following behind him. In the meantime, *Zia* Maria's heavy breathing began to subside.

She pushed away the water that was offered and beckoned him to help her stand. "Be careful," he said. "Don't do that too quickly."

"Don't be silly, Johnny!"

The man laughed. "You remember me!"

"Of course. What are you doing here?"

"I guess you don't know this, *Zia* Maria, but I work for Nick now."

Zia Maria looked at him with horror. "Nick? Oh, he big shot now. He got the bootleg." These phrases she uttered in English.

"Yes, I cannot tell a lie." Johnny said, smoothly. "My brother is a bootlegger. And he could use your help."

Long before a remarkable living could be made from bootlegging liquor, the Carpaccio family—patriarch Joe, wife Rosa, and their children, including Nicholas and John—had lived across the hall from *Zia* Maria and her own family. Joe and Rosa had passed away, their children had scattered to the four winds, but Nick Carpaccio kept the lease on the apartment and began to make his product there. While it had been months since *Zia* Maria had last seen Nick, she could understand why he was no longer around. So popular had his bootleg liquor become, he had to find another place to make it in the quantities clamored for. And, of course, with such celebrity came further demands on a bootlegger's time. It couldn't be wondered that her across-the-hall neighbor became an absentee neighbor.

Now she had it that Nick's younger brother had joined him in the business. It was a shame, but little wonder. In America, the children ran wild.

"Well… I pray for you and Nick. But I will help for your father's sake."

"Let me bring you to my brother. I'll take care of your groceries."

With *Zia* Maria leaning against Johnny as they walked, the two were soon standing before the doorway of Nick Carpaccio's apartment.

"He's sick," warned Johnny.

Undaunted, *Zia* Maria nodded and crossed herself. Johnny pushed the door open and took away her groceries.

The front room of Nick's apartment looked in many ways like *Zia* Maria's. It had the same plank floors, tall windows, and bare electric bulb. Other elements, however, indicated this apartment dweller had better means than his neighbors. A rug, for instance, resembling the fur of some exotic animal likely to be found in the Bronx Zoo. A Tiffany lamp on a low mahogany table, dripping in the sunshine that came through the windows. And a large brass bed on the back wall, this last item mounded with pillows and bright, floral bedding bespeaking the femininity of their arranger.

This feminine hand was not far off. She was, in fact, sitting next to the bed, while the reason she was there, the listless person beneath the covers, moaned softly.

She looked at *Zia* Maria with alarm. "Who are *you*?" this delicate-looking woman asked, her bleached hair and red cheeks trembling slightly. Fur flounced the collar and hem of the carelessly open coat she wore. She spoke with a working-class Brooklyn accent.

"*Zia* Maria, *buon giorno,*" came the reply.

"*Zia* who?" the woman asked.

Zia Maria was too fascinated by this friend of Nick's to respond. She guessed the woman to be his wife or girlfriend, though there was no way to know which without having a proper introduction. Deciding it was none of her business, *Zia* Maria set to work on her patient.

"Everyone meet?" Johnny asked on his return. "This is Nick's girl, Flo, and Flo, this is *Zia* Maria."

"She said *Zia* but that's all I heard," Flo countered.

"Well, that's her name. *Zia* Maria."

"Listen, Johnny, I told Nick none a' that eye-talian wid me. What's her name in English? What's she here for?"

"She's helping Nick."

"She a doctor?" Flo asked.

"No, a witch."

"A whhaat??!" Flo asked, her eyes enormous. "Fly a broomstick? That kinda witch?" She looked with concern from *Zia* Maria to Nick and back again.

"No, not that kind of witch," Johnny said. He sat now on a chair beside a window, opening the newspaper that had been tucked under his arm. Perfectly at ease, to Flo's eyes, with *Zia* Maria prodding his brother's throat and eyes and rolling up his pajama sleeve to look at his arm.

"Let her take care of him. It'll be fine."

"You brothers are crazy," Flo declared. Her coat slid from her shoulders to the chair as she came to her feet. "Can't you let me get a doctor? Hunter on Broome Street. He'll come in a jiffy."

"You do, you'll be sorry," Johnny responded.

"For the love of Pete, why not?" she demanded.

"Doctors are snitches," he said.

"Holy Moly, why do I let you talk me into things?" She began to pace, her hips swaying gently as Johnny took in her long legs.

"I persuade you." He answered, his eyes back on his Sports page.

Zia Maria, too, had stopped what she was doing to look at Flo's fine silhouette. She was grace itself, *Zia* Maria marveled, from her pearly shoulders to her willowy legs. But she had enough intuition to know when a woman—like this one—was no good. And now she had her proof. For when the sun embraced her form where Flo stood next to the window, *Zia* Maria saw she wore nothing beneath her flimsy dress.

Never mind that, *Zia* Maria told herself. She had work to do. Exchanging words with Johnny in dialect, she departed the flat. Soon she was back, carrying a bag, speaking again in that tongue that was foreign to Flo's ears.

Exasperated, Flo looked at them: "Didn't you hear me say…?"

"That's all she knows," Johnny said.

"Jesus Christ, she don't know English?"

"That's right," said Johnny. Then: "You may want to leave for this."

"Why's that?"

"She's going to bleed him."

"She…?"

At the table near the bed, *Zia* Maria tipped over a glass jar. A leech fell out of it. And then, after cutting a small, straight incision on Nick's skin with a small knife, she attached the creature to his arm.

"My Zia…" the invalid murmured.

Flo fainted.

"You have to be crazy to live in New York today." Lawrence was saying. Ann ensured she gave every sign of listening to him intently. "Crazy or criminal or a communist. And now the newspapers are getting into the act."

"He doesn't use a name or say where she lives," Ann said helpfully.

"Doesn't need to. Just the suspicion that anything but an inoculation can beat diphtheria is bound to add hundreds to the sick list and dozens to the coroner's report. I'd give my right arm to know how this guy could get away with this."

Ann was speechless, but not, for once, because of the acid tone in Lawrence's voice. Used to his dark outlook, she reasoned if it wasn't directed at her, her sanity and her job were safe. But she continued to believe Lawrence needed to cultivate more tolerance for the natural differences between people. Now, with this editorial, she began to wonder if his reputation as a bigot was catching up with him.

"Dr. Lawrence's muddled approach to this epidemic, as to epidemics in the past, is long on financial and manpower expenditure, short on results. While the number of diphtheria cases rises south of 14th Street, there is one hub below this divide with an acceptable level of infectious disease, and diphtheria in particular. This location is where Bleecker Street meets Mott, Elizabeth, and Mulberry Streets. The enclave has reported a handful of diphtheria cases since the epidemic began, vs. hundreds of cases in comparable localities.

Local intelligence attributes the low infection rate to a neighborhood woman claiming to be a witch. While the twentieth century mind may scoff at such superstitions, my sources say it would be unwise to dismiss the woman's methods. They work. This has been demonstrated by the few diphtheria cases, indeed, the few contagions of any kind, in the area where she practices."

"I have to find this woman," Dr. Lawrence brooded.

"No sense in that. We have our hands full with inoculations and Schick tests," said Ann.

"We can't let her give people a false sense of security," he persisted.

"Nobody even knows who she is."

"Not yet." He looked at Ann intently: "Now do you see what I mean about the ignorance of the wards south of 14th Street? They think superstition can protect them from epidemic disease. Think of what could happen if we had another pandemic like the Spanish Influenza and a woman like this one resisted our measures. Our jobs would be twice as hard."

Ann nodded. "What are you going to do?"

"I know people at the newspaper. I'll tell them I need to talk to this woman. The editor will do the rest."

Waking next to her patient's sickbed next morning, *Zia* Maria's eyes fell upon the jeweled hues of the bedspread. Beautiful. But she was where? She craned her neck to look around, only for her eyes to jerk back to the bed on hearing snoring beneath the covers. Who was there?

It came to her quite suddenly. That was Joe Carpaccio's son.

Zia Maria's next mental feat was to remember how Nick came to be so much better. It had been a long, eventful night. Other than recalling that, her mind was distressingly blank.

Ah…She had started by bleeding him.

Bleeding, as those in the healing arts knew, was contraindicated when the patient had fever, *except* when there was also a throat malady. The expanded girth of his neck told *Zia* Maria right away that Nick's throat and airways were swollen. Hence the need for the incision knife and the leeches.

After Flo fainted at the sight of her boyfriend being bled, *Zia* Maria decided to treat her patient using means that would spare Flo's delicate sensibilities. These included rubbing suet on his chest and boiling lemons for him to (reluctantly) ingest for the cough. For the fever, she wiped his forehead with a red sponge dipped in vinegar for hours.

When Johnny and Flo had departed for the evening, *Zia* Maria decided to revisit Nick's swollen air pipe. It was a good thing she did! She found the swelling severe enough to tie the Noose of the Quinsy—a string soaked with snake venom—

loosely around his neck. Then, lighting her oil lamp and rubbing some of the oil on her patient's wrist, she recited:

"Glands, little glands

The seven little brothers

The seven, the six,

The six, the five,

The five, the four,

The four, the three,

The three, the two,

The two, the one,

For one is not worth anything."

All while coaxing him to insert his fist into his mouth and breathe out, to exhale the sickness.

Finally, *Zia* Maria spoonfed her patient some of the luscious bone broth simmering on her stove for emergencies such as this one. Not long after her ministrations were finished, *Zia* Maria drifted to sleep beside the bed.

Now, with her patient snoring in the pink morning light, *Zia* Maria crept on snail's feet across the hall to prepare for her daytime clients.

The laundry shifting above their heads could be the banners belonging to ill-equipped band of revolutionaries, Ann couldn't help observing. There was no doubt the area was in need of a social crusader or progressivist, she mused, walking down Bleecker Street with Dr. Lawrence. The crowds in their morning rush to the subway or the commercial district barely cleared the pushcarts jamming the drab street, while the bright canopies and shop signs were a pale distraction from the grimy buildings and squalor below.

Ann and the doctor were, of course, visiting the person they now referred to as the Witch of Bleecker Street. Dr. Lawrence had made good his threat to visit the newspaper that ran the editorial criticizing the Division's efforts at curbing the diphtheria epidemic. Ann learned the editor demanded the name of the so-called witch from the reporter who wrote the piece. The man, having no desire to lose his living, gave the name directly. Now they were on their way to see a Mrs. Rosario Coniglio, who lived at 26 Bleecker Street.

For the entire train ride to the Bleecker Street Station, Ann listened grudgingly while Lawrence blasted the men, women, and children whose healthcare and safety they were sworn to protect. Soon, she could not help but pose the question she had wanted to ask him since starting with the Division.

"If you think so little of these people," she nodded at a family group outside an Italian grocery store, "why do you work for the NYC Board of Health? Must be someplace upstate or in New Jersey where you won't have to deal with immigrants."

Dr. Lawrence stopped walking. "Do I sound as if I dislike them?"

"Sometimes," Ann equivocated.

"I am sorry if that's how I sound. It's not dislike, it's more that I'm disappointed in today's immigrants." He elaborated: "I come from a long line of Puritans. The shining city on a hill, the New Jerusalem…you know. It's part of who I am."

"The Puritans came to New England to make a new start, just the way the Italians and Poles and Russian Jews are doing now."

"Yes, but my ancestors…*our* ancestors, Miss Becker…wanted to build a society that was better than the one they left. They didn't come here to benefit from the accomplishments of people who came before them."

"I don't know that the new immigrants are here to mooch. Most, as I understand it, are escaping conditions in their homelands—pogroms or starvation or forced conscription—and aren't infatuated with the American way of life."

"That tells you something, Miss Becker," said Lawrence, "when an Italian or Russian thinks they're on the same footing as Americans. And then, to add insult to injury, we have to teach the misfits of Europe how to live here."

"We, for the most part, are forcing that lesson," Ann replied.

"If it has to be forced, they need to go elsewhere."

"They're here," said Ann, "and not likely to stop coming."

"Well, if they insist on coming, they can't bite the hand that feeds them."

"Not make demands, you mean? Keep out of the way of *real Americans*, like you and me?" asked Ann, sardonically.

"Better than what they left," said Lawrence, with just as much bite.

Ann said something then she knew she would later regret saying:

"Half the world does not know how the other half lives.

The half on top cares little for the struggles,

less for the fate of those underneath,

so long as it's able to hold them there

and keep its own seat."

Dr. Lawrence spun on his heels to look at her. "Who said that?"

"Jacob Riis...'How the Other Half Lives.'"

"Let me remind you, Miss Becker, we're on Division business. We're not social reformers."

"Yessir," she said.

The two walked for some blocks without exchanging a word.

They finally stopped at the corner of Bleecker and Mott, where Lawrence gazed at his wristwatch. "We have five minutes to go, Miss Becker. I trust you'll spare me more moralizing until then," he said.

"Of course," she replied. "But what are we waiting for?"

"My interpreter," and Dr. Lawrence looked at Ann like someone who has outdone a rival. "It occurred to me, Miss Becker, that we need to have someone who speaks Mrs. Coniglio's language if we're going to get anywhere with her."

"The Italians have dozens of dialects. How do you know which one she speaks?"

"I don't," said Lawrence. "The newspaper editor is sending me someone who knows them all."

In a little while they were joined by a Dr. Rinaldo DiCarlo, a specialist in Southern Italian dialects from an upstate New York school. Ann and Dr. Lawrence did their best to follow the heavily accented English of this ardent and polite man.

As the three continued making their way to 26 Bleecker, Dr. Lawrence stopped his companions at the sandy patch where the children from Lina's building played. Here, he shared his hopes for being able to help the children on the playground, and all children from the city's slums. His attitude towards the youngsters, Ann quietly noted, was sharply at odds with his opinion of the parents.

"By getting vaccinated for diphtheria and other childhood illnesses, these kids won't have health problems related to a childhood bout with a disease they can be protected from. And what we can do for them doesn't stop there. Cleft lip and palate, asthma, thyroid disease, rickets, club foot, impetigo, not to mention poor nutrition and bad parenting, are all conditions we can eliminate. But we need cooperation, from the parents especially.

"This, too!" Lawrence declared on seeing Lina, alone on the curb in her characteristic manner. Grabbing the little girl, he turned her around, and, pointing to the birthmark, said: "Excise, stitch…gone. No more sitting on the playground alone." Lina pulled her arm free and ran away, crying.

DiCarlo and Miss Becker exchanged glances.

"It's not the first time a Department of Health has called me," DiCarlo said, in a bid to change the subject. "Upstate there are enclaves where people speak mostly an Italian or Sicilian dialect. Sometimes I can make out the dialect, if it's widely used. Other times, we get a little help from the neighbors."

Ann smiled at Dr. DiCarlo warmly, while Dr. Lawrence assumed a look of grave concern.

Once anointed with Oil of Amber Essence, the white candle burning in *Zia* Maria's kitchen sparked with a new intensity. The oil had not been easy to find, but the ingredient was vital for *Zia* Maria's spell of protection for Lina. How she had bargained with the grocer to get a good price for it. In the end, he let it go for a song, admitting there were fewer customers for the rare ingredient, because there were fewer witches.

Not easy to obtain, but critical for keeping Lina safe, as was the tall, fat, white candle on the table. When she had these necessities, along with the lock of Lina's hair, *Zia* Maria had asked the building superintendent to write "protection" and "Lina" on some paper. *Zia* Maria carved the words into the candle wax with a nail, then tied the hair around the candle. After this, it was only left to apply the oil and burn the candle for ten minutes a day until it had melted down. And then little Lina would be out of harm's way.

While the candle was burning, *Zia* Maria put away the basins, pots, cloths, and ointments she had used for treating her morning clients. In the middle of this activity, she heard a knock at the door. Another neighbor, she assumed, with a problem or malady, come to seek her counsel. But when she answered, she was startled to see two men and a woman whom she had never set eyes on, all looking very serious. And she tried to recall what she may have done to bring such somber faces to her door.

Her panic was somewhat dispelled when Dr. DiCarlo spoke to her in Italian: *"Buon giorno. Dove sono Signora Coniglio, per favore?"*

"Si, si..." *Zia* Maria replied. *"Io sono Signora Coniglio."*

Unfortunately, the two did not get much farther than this. With her initial greeting, *Zia* Maria spoke all of the Italian she knew. Every time Dr. DiCarlo tried speaking in a dialect he thought she might understand, but didn't, *Zia* Maria became worried and agitated. This exercise in futility continued while Ann and Dr. Lawrence remained in the hallway, watching.

Not much time passed before *Zia* Maria's neighbors on the hall began peering from behind their doors, curiosity, for once, overcoming a native fear of strangers. One of them, the teen-ager Louie, was enterprising enough to approach the group. Soon he was the acting intermediary for *Zia* Maria and her visitors.

"They are from the Board of Health, *Zia* Maria. Dr. Lawrence here wants to know if you are treating people for diphtheria."

After exchanging more words with her, the young man turned to the visitors. "She said she treated one man, and now he's well."

Dr. Lawrence took a breath and squared his shoulders: "She is to treat no one else. Diphtheria is a contagious disease that can kill someone her age. We're going to start inoculating everyone in the building…"

The young man repeated the doctor's words so that *Zia* Maria understood. She responded, and Louie turned back to repeat her words in English. "She wants to know why you doctors have not been able to stop the fevers."

His face stony, Dr. Lawrence replied: "There is a diphtheria *inoculation*. There should not be, and from the moment we give the inoculation, *there will not be* any more diphtheria. The fact that there were fevers—any fevers at all—shows that precautions were not taken to prevent the disease."

Another exchange between Louie and *Zia* Maria. And her reply: "The fever attacked *Zia* Maria's patient because he had a severe shock. She learned from him that he was disappointed in love. The resulting fever was accompanied by a cough and a swelling of the throat. She treated him, and now he is well. There is no need for your help."

Dr. Lawrence's stony look was replaced by anger: "Tell Mrs. Coniglio she can be jailed for practicing medicine without a license."

Zia Maria's response, and Louie's interpretation of it, was swift: "She was not using doctor's medicine. She was using her own medicine from the wise women she knew in Sicily. You would do just as well to use her cures and spells of healing. She knows that sometimes your needles—inoculations—are as dangerous as the illness. Three children here died from them last year."

Lawrence was now clearly enraged, and *Zia* Maria's neighbors heard his reply from behind their half-closed doors: "It was a bad batch of the toxin anti-toxin that killed those children. Good inoculations do not kill people. They prevent illness caused by over-crowding and poor hygiene. Not by being disappointed in love!"

Zia Maria didn't wait for the translation: "Her good magic has protected everyone in the building, save one, from the diphtheria," Louie relayed.

"You listen to me, you…" Lawrence was going say "stupid little witch doctor," but Ann interrupted.

"Dr. Lawrence! Don't you think we've done all we can do here?"

He nodded circumspectly. "Yes, yes. Nothing more we can do."

Lawrence, Ann, and DiCarlo walked to the stairs quietly, their remaining shreds of dignity carried in tow.

Zia Maria groaned when she found her daughter, Angela, looking at the letter the Board of Health had sent to her. It was her intention to burn it before Angela or anybody else could see it, but now it was too late. While Angela read the Board of Health correspondence, *Zia* Maria watched the increasing dismay settling into the lines on her daughter's forehead.

"Have you been talking to the Board of Health?" Angela asked.

"*Si, si.*" said *Zia* Maria. They were conversing in *Zia* Maria's dialect.

"Some people from the Board of Health…" *Zia* Maria pretended to be busy with what she had on the stove, "…talked to me".

"About…practicing medicine without a license?"

The older woman stopped stirring her effusion and looked down. Even a fool could see she was trying to evade her daughter's eyes. Tired of the ploy, *Zia* Maria put her wooden spoon on the stove and nodded. Barely.

"It says here they can fine you. $100.00 for every instance. You can't afford that kind of money, Mama."

Nodding again, *Zia* Maria looked at her hands, now resting on her apron front.

"I'll take this home with me. Perhaps I can find a way to get you out of this," said Angela.

Soon after returning from visiting *Zia* Maria, Lawrence enlisted the help of the police sanitary inspector for the Ward, requesting him to detail sanitary violations at 26 Bleecker Street and the surrounding streets, tenements, shops, and alleys. Lawrence himself typed the first violation letter to Mrs. Coniglio, warning her to stop practicing medicine without a license. While he didn't have approval to send it, he thought under the circumstances it wasn't needed. Now he knew he was correct. Before him were the numbers for last month's diphtheria cases, showing that cases had doubled.

"Yes," Ann intoned, "but there were no cases for 26 Bleecker. Nor for most of the buildings surrounding it."

"Which means nothing." Lawrence slammed the drawer of the file cabinet where he was stowing the report. "Just a week or two—at most—and they'll have diphtheria, too."

"I'm not so certain," Ann countered. "The condition of that building is quite good compared to other tenements I've visited. No holes in the walls, no debris, no water beneath the building. And the communal sinks and water closets pristine."

"That doesn't mean we should discourage residents from getting inoculated."

"I don't think so, either. But we can learn a thing or two about how to prevent diphtheria from residents who live where it hasn't spread."

"We can't do that at 26 Bleecker because they'll say it's because of that…witch doctor. And we can't leave them with the impression they're safe from infection."

"Of course not," said Ann. "But we want to understand why the building has avoided becoming the incubator the rest of the Ward is. Later, after the epidemic, we can provide guidelines to all the Wards on how to avoid contagion. We don't even have to mention the address. Or Mrs. Coniglio."

"Alright, alright." said Lawrence. He wasn't convinced. Only worn down. "I'll ask the police sanitary inspector to talk to the superintendent at the building."

He put on his hat to leave for the day. "I'll see you tomorrow."

Miss Becker, Dr. Lawrence ruminated while taking the elevator to the lobby, was the most intelligent, efficient, and amiable female colleague he had worked with in years. But she had the tenacity of a junkyard dog who hadn't eaten for a week. Time and again he was tempted to tell her to go back to Hartford. He didn't, because good employees were hard to find, but he didn't think it would kill her to admit he was running the show once in a while.

After a short walk and subway ride, Dr. Lawrence stood outside the cellar of a MacDougal Street tenement. Having knocked on the cellar door three times, he soon was seated at the inside bar, whiskey and soda in hand. Prohibition be damned, he mused. This was one place he wouldn't run into Miss Becker.

While Miss Becker was the last person he wanted to encounter, Lawrence was more than happy to see Jim Martell, City Editor for the New York Beacon. The two men sat together after exchanging greetings.

"I hear you went on a hunting expedition today." Martell made sure that he kept at least as well-informed as his reporters.

"Did you know there are witch doctors in New York?" said Lawrence, by way of answer.

"Witch doctors? You mean the kind that wear the headdress and do a medicine dance?"

"That's a medicine man," Lawrence chided. "No headdress. She looked like somebody's grandmother."

"Probably is someone's grandmother. What'd you get out of her?"

"Something about diphtheria being caused by being disappointed in love."

Martell laughed. "Oh wow. She's the Real McCoy. Well, did she say she'll stop?"

"No."

"You tell her she can't stand in the way of people getting inoculated?"

"Didn't get that far."

"Geez", said Martell. "Tough break. I don't know what to say. You don't want to mess with an Italian grandmother. Get too rough, and you'll have egg on your face."

The two drank in silence. And then: "My reporter found out she treated one case of diphtheria. Was it a kid?" Martell asked.

"No. The building superintendent told Ann Becker it was a guy named Nick Carpaccio."

"Nick Carpaccio. Hmmm." And Martell scratched his chin. "Hey…I wonder if that's the Nick Carpaccio I heard about?"

Dr. Lawrence signaled the bartender for another drink. "Don't know. Who is he?"

"A Missing Person report was filed on a bootlegger who wound up getting pulled out of the river. Those guys don't rat on each other too often, but this one had a friend who did. He put the finger on another bootlegger, this character Carpaccio, and now the cops are looking for him. If this woman nursed him, the police could have a case on her for aiding and abetting."

"You don't say?" Lawrence smiled. His day had just taken a hairpin turn for the better.

Examining the birthmark on Lina's face, *Zia* Maria could now see it stretched from above the little girl's cheekbone, across the hollow, down almost to her jawline. Looking still closer, *Zia* Maria saw hair—the short, fine hairs on a mouse—in the middle of the mark.

Lina bore the exam patiently from where she sat on *Zia* Maria's kitchen table, all the time relishing the thumb nestled in her mouth. With patience and tenderness, *Zia* Maria rubbed the dark patch, reciting *Pater Nosters*, *Ave Marias*, and any other prayer or invocation she thought might spirit the stain off Lina's face.

The old woman had never seen a mole quite like this one, but she did know birthmarks were the result of a craving the mother had while carrying. The cure was to apply the craved food to the mark. While it was true Lina's birthmark at first glance resembled a smear of paint or tar, *Zia* Maria decided it had the essential shape of a zucchini or cucumber. Now she pressed slices of both on Lina's face.

It was evident Lina's needs were not only physical. Her ease in accompanying *Zia* Maria to her flat hinted at neglect, as did her need for affection. She would make it a habit, *Zia* Maria resolved, to stop by the makeshift playground to see the child more often. Perhaps little Lina would even like to help with her clients, to fetch things and carry water.

For *Zia* Maria's client list had become only more numerous in the days since the Board of Health visited. More numerous, too, were the letters from that agency, a pile of them, in fact, on the table near where Lina sat.

Zia Maria would wait for Angela to decide what to do with them. It wasn't that the letters did not concern her. It was more that events in her life had opened her eyes to the futility of working too hard to change fate. She believed nothing happened without God's will directing it to happen. This being the case, no matter what, she was in God's hands. Knowing this was enough for *Zia* Maria to have peace of mind.

And now it was time to take Lina home. Grasping the child's hand in her own, the two were almost at the stairway landing when they came face-to-face with the building superintendent and a policeman.

"Are you Mrs. Maria Coniglio?" the policeman asked. The superintendent repeated the question so *Zia* Maria could understand.

"Si."

"I have to ask you to come with me to the police station for questioning."

Looking back on the incident, *Zia* Maria would chuckle when recalling the chaos that followed this request. She immediately dropped Lina's hand, gesturing for the girl to depart. Then she blurted plaintively that someone needed to tell her daughter where she was going. She hadn't counted on Lina's quick reaction to her plight, for once free, the little girl whisked down the stairs, shouting at the top of her lungs that the police were taking Zia Maria away. The news would get to her daughter even before her shoes hit the sidewalk!

So it was that the old woman headed for the police station. She could not know how long she would be gone, or that her life would never be the same.

A harmless old woman. That's what the Sergeant O'Bryan saw in *Zia* Maria, standing before his desk. It was astounding to him that the Health Department claimed she aided and abetted a fugitive and practiced medicine without a license. Ignorant of the law as she probably was—for O'Bryan found that most people were ignorant in this regard—he believed every citizen over the age of majority should be held responsible for his (or, in this case, her) actions.

"Mrs. Coniglio, can you tell me where you were on March 12?" The station interpreter repeated the question.

"She doesn't know," said the interpreter.

O'Bryan sucked in his breath. This was going to be harder than he thought. Bending over his desk to put her reply in his notes, he saw a shadow darken the papers before him. He looked up to see *Zia* Maria's daughter.

"Why is my mother here?" Angela asked.

"Practicing medicine without a license. Aiding and abetting a fugitive from justice."

Angela looked at her *Zia* Maria. "We're going to need a lawyer."

Angela watched in disbelief when her mother started preparing for her next day's clients after they returned to her flat.

"Mama, I don't think you understand what's happening. What do you think you're doing with that wool? What are you making on the stove?"

She had to take care of the people in the building, *Zia* Maria told Angela, so they would not get sick. The old people needed her help with their gout and arthritis. And the diphtheria was going around.

"Helping people is why the police went after you, Mama."

"No, no…" *Zia* Maria objected.

"Yes, yes. You have to stay out of trouble so I can find you a lawyer. You were arraigned and Sergeant O'Bryan set a date for your court trial…remember? You are in my custody until then. Look at all these letters saying you're practicing medicine without a license. You have to stop doing the things that get you into trouble. Do you understand me, Mama?"

Zia Maria put aside the things in her hands and looked down. After a moment of indecision, she nodded her head, slowly.

She would spend much of her time before the trial with Lina. Instead of making plasters and potions alone in her kitchen, *Zia* Maria took the child with her shopping, sat on the playground to keep a protective eye on her while she played, even had her over for meals. As the bond between them grew more robust—with Lina's eyes lighting up and a smile kissing her mouth whenever she was around—*Zia* Maria began to look on the girl as her own dear godchild. More importantly, from this time on, she rarely heard Lina cry.

If one of her former clients came to the door of her flat or saw her elsewhere, *Zia* Maria made excuses for why she could not treat them. Not now, she said. Later. She meant it, for *Zia* Maria could not imagine being deprived of the healing magic she had practiced for decades and with which she had helped so many people. She wouldn't mind for herself. But her clients—ah, they would feel the absence of her healing touch most acutely.

"Hear ye, hear ye, hear ye! The Criminal Court for New York County, State of New York, is now in session. All rise for Judge Dexter Bartleby III."

As she rose precariously from her chair at the Defense Table, *Zia* Maria's legs began to wobble. Her new shoes were a tad larger, their heels a little higher, than she liked. Only the supporting arm extended to her by Elijah Loew—her lawyer from the Legal Aid Society—kept her from falling onto the courtroom's tiled floor. Loew was equally responsible for restoring her view when her new hat slid down over her eyes as she stood reciting the Pledge of Allegiance with the rest of the

Court. He pushed the cloche back up to her forehead and helped her resume her chair while everyone was sitting down again.

Not only *Zia* Maria*'s* shoes and hat were new. For this, her first and only time in a courtroom, she wore a store-bought dress, stockings, and new undergarments, too. Her plain black dress was decorated with the gold cross she had worn on her wedding day and an American flag pin from Woolworth's five-and-dime store. Everything—shoes, hat, dress, stockings, and the flag pin most of all—had been carefully selected and bought for the sake of making a good impression, as that nice Mr. Loew explained.

"Do you understand the charges against you, Mrs. Coniglio?" She knew to listen for these words, although she was a little unclear on why they said she was doing what a doctor did. It was not true. She went along with it anyway. The main thing, as both her daughter and her lawyer said, was not to make things worse.

"Yes."

"How do you plead?"

"My client pleads Not Guilty to both charges," replied Mr. Loew.

Zia Maria sat down.

The Assistant District Attorney took the floor. "Ladies and gentlemen of the jury: The defendant in this case is Mrs. Maria Coniglio, charged with aiding and abetting a fugitive from justice and practicing medicine without a license. Mrs. Coniglio has led a life—some would say an average life—similar to thousands of women in this great metropolis. She is a mother, a church goer, a housewife, a grandmother.

"While I have no wish to discredit the defendant, I want the jury to consider that few of these thousands—mothers, churchgoers, grandmothers, just like Mrs. Coniglio—will ever face the allegations she does today.

"I also want you to consider the importance New York City places on upholding the law, no matter the alleged lawbreaker's country of origin, or how long they have lived here. And to remember the Board of Health—filing the charge of practicing medicine without a license—came into being to benefit individuals such as Mrs. Coniglio.

"The city did, in fact, transform itself to protect and respond to a population of immigrants—like Mrs. Coniglio—who have everything to gain from our great democracy, and the true American ideals of tolerance, fortitude, and manifest progress…"

"Mr. Moffat—this is not the time for a campaign speech," said the Judge, banging his gavel. He, and most others in the room, were aware of rumors that Assistant District Attorney Moffat would run in the next mayoral election.

"Yes, Your Honor." Moffat sat down.

With the judge nodding in Mr. Loew's direction, *Zia Maria's* lawyer took the floor.

"Ladies and gentlemen of the jury: I want to introduce to you Mrs. Maria Coniglio, a widow, 76 years old, who came from her native Sicily to the United States five decades ago. She and her deceased husband raised eight children here in Lower Manhattan. She never had a job, speaks no English, lives in humble circumstances.

"I tell you these things to call your attention to the exemplary life Mrs. Coniglio has led. She has never, until now, been in trouble with the law. Yet, Mrs. Coniglio stands before you with serious charges leveled at her. I hope to convince you any blame she bears can be excused by her high motives and the mitigating events that led to these charges. My client has lived her life solely for the good of others. It's due to this unending devotion to her fellow men and women that she is in her predicament today."

Picking up a folder, he walked toward the jury.

"Here are glowing letters and testimonials from my client's family, friends, and neighbors. I draw your attention especially to a testimony from her parish priest, who commends Maria Coniglio for her charity and love for church and family." He left the folder with the jury foreman.

"Your witness, Mr. Moffat," said the Judge.

"Your Honor, I wish to call Miss Florence McClure to the witness stand."

Zia Maria saw the woman from Nick's apartment sweep into the courtroom. Flo's rouge was lighter, her heels lower, and, of course, today she wore underwear. But in all other respects it was the same person.

"Miss McClure, can you identify the woman at the defense table?"

"Well…I can't say her name. But I seen her before."

"Where did you see her?"

"At 26 Bleecker Street, Apartment 5C, on March 12."

"What were you doing there?"

"I came with Nick Carpaccio and his brother Johnny. Nick was there cause he was sick and needed a place to stay. She was nursin'…" Flo became flustered…"I mean, bein' a doctor to Nick."

She turned to the Judge: "Nick used to be my fiancée, but not no more."

"Answer only the questions that are put to you, Miss McClure," Bartleby responded.

"Why did Mr. Carpaccio choose this location to get well?" Moffat asked.

"Because the cops were tailin' him, and Nick thought they wouldn't look there."

"Did Mrs. Coniglio know Mr. Carpaccio was wanted by the police?"

"Yes," said Flo.

"How do you know this?"

"Nick tole me," she answered.

"That's all, Miss McClure. You can step down." When Loew indicated he had no questions for Flo, Moffat told the Judge he had no more witnesses for the prosecution.

Loew came forward. "The Defense calls Mr. John Carpaccio to the stand," he said.

Zia Maria gripped the Rosary beads that were on the Defense Table before her. The Carpaccio family never needed her prayers more than now.

"Can you identify the woman at the defense table?" Loew asked Johnny.

"Yes, *Zia* Maria. Uh…Mrs. Coniglio."

"Did you see Mrs. Coniglio on March 12?"

"Yes."

"Under what circumstances did you meet her on that day?"

"We were at 26 Bleecker Street, Apartment 5C, where my brother was sick. I asked her to see him."

"Did Mrs. Coniglio know your brother was wanted in connection with an alleged murder?"

"No."

"Did you or your brother at any time tell Mrs. Coniglio he was wanted by the police?"

"No."

"Miss McClure said your brother told Mrs. Coniglio the police wanted him."

"That's wrong."

Moffat stepped up to cross-examine Johnny.

"Mr. Carpaccio, you've been found guilty of aiding and abetting a fugitive from justice. Why should we believe you, someone who assisted an individual wanted in connection with a murder?" asked Moffatt.

"Because what I'm saying is the truth," Johnny replied.

"That's all," said Moffatt.

At this time, the Judge asked for the Court's attention: "I have here intelligence that Nick Carpaccio is in police custody," said Bartleby. The courtroom instantly came alive with chatter that ended when he banged his gavel.

"With this development, the court has decided not to pursue the case of aiding and abetting, and that charge has been dropped. We'll proceed now with the charge of practicing medicine without a license, starting with witnesses for the prosecution."

On hearing what the Judge had said from the court interpreter, *Zia* Maria didn't know whether to be happy or sad.

She did know to grasp her Rosary beads tightly, silently asking the Lord to grant guidance and wisdom to Nick, that prodigal son of her old friend, Joe Carpaccio.

"The court calls Dr. John Lawrence to the Witness Stand," said Moffatt. Once he was seated on the stand, Lawrence was asked his name and place of work: "I am Dr. John Edwin Lawrence, Director of the Division of Disease Prevention at the NYC Board of Health."

"What has caught your attention about Mrs. Maria Coniglio in your position with the Board of Health, Dr. Lawrence?"

"Well," and Dr. Lawrence spread his hands as if to ask where to begin. "Mrs. Coniglio thinks she can stem the recent diphtheria epidemic that has taken 600 lives in this city to date. She is known to have used her own slipshod practices to 'treat', if I may use that term loosely, at least one case of diphtheria, and that is the case of Nicholas Carpaccio."

"Objection, your honor. My client never claimed she could end the diphtheria epidemic," Loew protested.

"Sustained," said the Judge.

"Your honor, we're trying to establish that Mrs. Coniglio has an exaggerated idea of her own abilities. We'll get to the reasons directly," Moffatt rebutted.

"Proceed," said the Judge.

"What do you believe can happen when a person with limited—or in the case of Mrs. Coniglio, **no**—medical training, claims she can cure a disease as serious as diphtheria?" Assistant DA Moffatt continued.

Dr. Lawrence placed his palms on the witness stand before him. "False hope. The unsupported belief that a few mumbled prayers and some cuttings from the side of the road will stop a contagion that can wipe out an unprotected population. We all remember the Spanish Influenza pandemic…"

"Just stick to the point, Dr. Lawrence," the Judge suggested.

"What suggests to you Mrs. Coniglio is spreading false hope?" Moffatt asked.

"Statistics." Dr. Lawrence answered.

"What do the numbers say?"

"The Board of Health's drive to inoculate the Lower Manhattan wards against diphtheria has been an unqualified success except in a few random areas."

"Where are those areas?" Moffatt asked, as the bailiff pulled down the courtroom's wall map of Lower Manhattan.

"Certain areas of the East Side and around the Bowery. And where Mott, Elizabeth, and Mulberry Streets run into Bleecker Street. The numbers show an inoculation rate for these areas of 5% or lower, while the average inoculation rate for Lower Manhattan is 50% or higher."

"What do the buildings in that last area you mentioned have in common other than their low inoculation rate?"

"These are the areas where Mrs. Maria Coniglio 'practices.'"

"What do you mean when you say she 'practices'? Does Mrs. Coniglio have a medical degree? Has she worked in a hospital or a clinic or for a doctor, ever?"

Lawrence smirked as he answered: "The people in her building would refer to her—not at all euphemistically—as a witch."

The Judge sat up at attention. "A witch? The kind they burned at the stake?"

"No," Lawrence and Moffat both said at the same time.

"She practices a primitive form of folk medicine using prayers, herbs, and religious artifacts—pictures, crosses, beads, and the like—common in the land of her birth," said Lawrence.

"For example?"

"Well, when I went to talk her out of practicing these 'healing arts', she told me Mr. Carpaccio's brush with diphtheria was caused by…" He looked around with amusement…"being disappointed in love."

Everyone in the courtroom laughed. Everyone but *Zia Maria*, who looked about with puzzlement that turned to indignity when the interpreter translated the remark for her.

"But what did she do to treat Mr. Carpaccio?"

"That I cannot say, because I found myself in the position of having to defend our modern practices against her idea of medical practice…uhh…prayers and herbs, etc.," More laughter in the courtroom.

The Judge pounded the gavel: "Order!"

"I see, Doctor," said Moffatt. He returned his attention to the map, and, with a pointer, he circled where Bleecker, Mott, Elizabeth, and Mulberry Streets came together. "This is the area with an inoculation rate of no more than 5%?"

"Yes," said Dr. Lawrence.

"Where does Mrs. Coniglio live?"

"26 Bleecker, Apartment 5C."

"Your witness," Moffat said to Loew.

Mr. Loew put down the papers he had been examining. "How many times have you met Mrs. Coniglio?" he asked Lawrence.

"Just once."

"What made you decide to visit her?"

"I'm not sure what you mean."

"A woman out of tens of thousands living in Lower Manhattan grabs your attention. How did that happen?"

Again, that gesture with the open hands: "We were inoculating the city against diphtheria—especially the Lower Wards where contagions are rife because of overcrowding. I had to ask Mrs. Coniglio not to discourage the people she 'treated' from getting inoculated."

"We've established that, Dr. Lawrence. But how did you learn Mrs. Coniglio was treating people?"

"Answer the question," the Judge instructed.

There was a pause.

"Hearsay."

"Thank-you, Dr. Lawrence."

Moffat walked to the witness stand. "You can step down, Dr. Lawrence. My next witness is Miss Florence McClure."

Flo rose from where she sat, not far from Johnny, and walked with graceful strides to the witness stand. *Zia* Maria was again struck by her beauty. Still, she thought Nick was being dealt a lucky card if his present troubles brought his relationship with her to an end.

"Miss McClure, can you tell us what happened at 26 Bleecker Street, Apartment 5C, on March 12?" Moffat asked.

"Well, I was sitting next to the bed with Nick. Not *in* the bed…*near* the bed. And in comes Johnny and this *Zia* person…"

"*Zia?*" Moffat asked, puzzled.

The court interpreter spoke: "*Zia* means 'aunt'."

"I see," said Moffat. "Immaterial what she's called. The defendant was there, Miss McClure?"

"She was there alright. Slicin' Nick open with a knife…"

"Do you mean to say she operated on him?" asked the Judge.

"No… that is… I ain't sure. Cause that's when I fainted," Flo answered. "But there was no scar after I came to, 'ceptin' on his arm."

"I see."

"And what did Mrs. Coniglio do after she cut the arm, Miss McClure?" asked Moffat.

"She took out a jar of leeches and dropped one on him. That's when I fainted."

"That'll do, Miss McClure," said Moffat. And then: "Your witness, Mr. Loew."

As usual, Loew took his time going to the witness stand. "Miss McClure, what were the results of these—unusual—actions by Mrs. Coniglio?"

"He got well," she said. Then, looking at Moffat sheepishly: "Better."

"Thank-you, Miss McClure. No further questions."

With Moffat indicating he had no more prosecution witnesses, the Judge invited Loew to call his witnesses for the defense. The first of these was Johnny.

"Mr. Carpaccio," began Mr. Loew. "Were you present when Mrs. Coniglio performed the actions Miss McClure alleges?"

"Yes, Mrs. Coniglio bled my brother."

"What else did she do?"

"Brought down the fever with vinegar, boiled lemons and gave him some, rubbed lard on him, prayed…that's all I remember."

Zia Maria crossed herself with relief, thankful Johnny wasn't there when she used the Noose of Quinsy for Nick's swollen airways. She wouldn't have wanted to explain what it was or how it was created to the Judge.

"And the next day he was well?"

Johnny nodded. "The fever was gone."

"What do you attribute this to?"

"To *Zia* Maria. For decades I've seen her turn around sicknesses going around in that building without help from anyone," said Johnny, while Dr. Lawrence reddened visibly. "She cures lots of things: flu, scarlet fever, measles, colds, broken bones, rheumatism, gout, skin disease. You name it."

"Thank-you, Mr. Carpaccio."

With Johnny's testimony ended, the Judge called Mr. Loew to the bench. Speaking in a low voice, Bartleby asked Loew to explain his strategy: "What point are you trying to make, Mr. Loew? That the defendant knows some rudimentary medical practices? You can say that about anyone who raised eight children. The question is: did she practice medicine without a license?"

"My next witness will get us closer to that answer, your Honor."

"See that they do," warned Bartleby.

With this, Loew called Ann Becker to the stand. On hearing Ann's name being called for the defense, Moffatt and Lawrence looked at each other with dismay. Jumping from his chair, Moffat stormed over to the Judge's Bench.

"Miss Becker works for the Board of Health, who has brought this suit against Mrs. Coniglio." he declared.

"True enough," said Mr. Loew. "She is entering these proceedings as a hostile witness."

Ann's misgivings about testifying, very likely tangled up with worries about her job, were evident as she walked to the Witness Stand. Yet, she seemed calmer on taking the stand, perhaps even reconciled to her part in the unfolding drama. Many who were in Court said later that day they thought there was an undertone of relief in her words.

"Miss Becker…what happened when you and Dr. Lawrence went to 26 Bleecker to talk to Mrs. Coniglio?"

"Mrs. Coniglio told us through an interpreter her diagnosis of Mr. Nick Carpaccio's condition."

"What was it?"

"She said Mr. Carpaccio took a fever. He also had a cough and a swelling of the throat, all consistent with a diagnosis of diphtheria. Unfortunately, we never saw Mr. Nicholas Carpaccio, and so we could not take a throat culture. Maybe he had something other than diphtheria."

"What do you think of the way she treated Mr. Carpaccio's illness?"

"Bloodletting is unusual in this day and age, but not as rare as people think. Mrs. Coniglio probably brought the practice over with her from Sicily. Soup, especially bone broth, is known to have curative qualities and to help with hydration during fevers. Vinegar has been used to bring down a high temperature for millennia. Boiled lemon gives patients a good amount of Vitamin C, breaks up congestion, and creates saliva to aid hydration. Saying prayers to restore somebody to good health can hardly be a bad thing. As far as rubbing lard on the chest goes...I don't know how that works."

Loew scratched his head. "You said nobody in this courtroom can positively identify what Mr. Carpaccio suffered from. But let's suppose he had a mild case of diphtheria. From what you've said, there's a good chance Mrs. Coniglio's treatments helped him. Maybe it was exactly what was needed to short circuit the infection," Loew finished.

"Would you agree, Miss Becker?" asked the Judge.

"Yes," she said.

"But these *are* home remedies, aren't they? In other words, nothing a doctor would do with a patient," Loew suggested.

"Yes," Ann agreed.

"Then she ain't a witch?" asked Flo, loud enough for everyone to hear.

"Miss McClure, you are out of order!" barked the Judge.

"If I may be so bold as to answer Miss McClure's question, your Honor," said Ann.

"Yes, Miss Becker, you may," the Judge sighed.

"Whether or not we call Mrs. Coniglio a witch hinges on our own definition of what a witch is and what they are capable of doing. Certainly, she is not a witch of the wild imaginings of book and stage and screen. That is, there is nothing scary or demented or unnatural in the healing arts she practices.

"Those archetypes are based on the popular idea of witches as practitioners of black magic. We haven't gotten into what, if any, magic Mrs. Coniglio uses. But based on what was said here and in testimonials, I'd guess her dedication to doing good suggests Mrs. Coniglio practices white magic only."

At that, the jury and most others in the courtroom turned to look at *Zia* Maria. Unable to follow the proceedings, she had dozed off some time ago. With the court's attention turned to his client, Mr. Loew leaned over to rouse her gently. Her eyes fluttered open, and, looking about to see that everyone was watching her, *Zia* Maria smiled engagingly.

That smile was returned by many.

Judge Bartleby banged his gavel. "This court will recess for lunch."

Zia Maria never had such a pleasant lunch. Her frankfurter from a stand outside the courthouse was one of the most delectable meals of her life, more so after Mr. Loew told her and Angela the case was going well.

The sky was a brilliant blue, with wrens and sparrows and robins darting in and out of the splendid elms burrowed in the sidewalk, while squirrels and pigeons competed for the crumbs falling from the food stands. Here and there, *Zia* Maria saw some of the people from the courtroom who had been sitting in the wooden box across from the Judge's Bench. Regretfully, Johnny was not able to join *Zia* Maria and her daughter, but he did take the time to kiss her cheek before the bailiff led him from the courtroom.

On the other side of the courthouse steps stood the lovely woman, Miss Becker, and the brute, Dr. Lawrence. Unlike Miss Becker, who balanced competence with love, *Zia* Maria guessed Lawrence lived for the power of his position. "Hell is full of lawyers, doctors, professors, pharmacists, and judges" it was said. This, without a doubt, was Lawrence's fate, too.

Zia Maria wouldn't be surprised to learn Ann was just then coming to the same conclusion.

"Miss Becker," Dr. Lawrence said, walking to where she sat, "remind me I need to reassign you with the janitors. You have a certain facility with a load of crap."

"If you're referring to my testimony, I was subpoenaed and had to testify. Besides, you know these lawyers. When Moffatt cross-examines me, he'll turn everything I said around."

"Maybe," Dr. Lawrence granted. "Unless you painted too rosy a picture of our sainted witch doctor."

Losing her temper, Miss Becker snarled: "I will never understand how you can have such a vendetta against a poor old woman like Mrs. Coniglio, who, at her age, may not be alive in a year, for all we know."

"I suggest, Miss Becker," Dr. Lawrence countered, "you'd do better to think of the countless little children who *may not be alive in a year*, if that *poor old woman* has her way."

He threw his hot dog wrapper in a nearby garbage can and walked away.

Just then Mr. Loew was rejoining *Zia* Maria and her daughter on the other side of the courthouse steps. "I think I bought your mother her ticket out of jail," he told Angela.

"He'll drop the charges?" asked Angela, who knew Mr. Loew had been conferring with the Judge in his chambers. She blurted this very thing to her mother in dialect, who almost dropped her Coke with excitement.

"Yes, that's right," said Loew. "She just has to promise not to 'practice her unique brand of medicine'—what the Judge called it—anymore."

Angela turned to her mother and repeated Mr. Loew's statement, grimly.

The look of steel on *Zia* Maria's face astonished the lawyer.

"She won't do it?"

"I'll try to talk her into it," said Angela, but her tone was doubtful.

"When? Court's in session now."

Angela could do no more than shake her head, while she gently helped *Zia* Maria get to her feet and up the courthouse steps.

Both lawyers were asked to approach the bench once everyone had returned to their places in the courtroom. When Judge Bartleby began to talk about dropping the charges in return for *Zia* Maria's promise to stop treating people with her healing arts, Mr. Loew said she was not interested. "I don't believe my client understands the seriousness of the charges against her. She has deferred to accept your offer," he admitted.

"Perhaps you should let her approach the bench," said the Judge.

"I don't know if that's advisable. My client does not want the charges dropped," said Moffat.

Judge Bartleby shook his head in annoyance. "That's how they want it…this court is back in session." He banged his gavel.

"Your job," he was still speaking to the lawyers at the bench, "is to prove or disprove that Mrs. Coniglio was practicing medicine without a license. Would you like to cross-examine the last witness, Mr. Moffat?"

"Yes, your Honor," said Moffat.

With Ann re-established on the witness stand, Moffat walked to the center of the room.

"Based on the testimony you gave in this courtroom, are you telling me Mrs. Coniglio was not menacing the public health by practicing her 'healing arts' on her neighbors in and around 26 Bleecker Street?"

"Yes," said Ann.

"So, somebody has diphtheria, they knock on Mrs. Coniglio's door, she makes everything alright? That how it goes?"

"I'm not saying she can cure everything…"

"Where do you draw the line between the conditions she can handle and the ones she should lay off treating?" Moffat shot back.

"We have to know what her strengths are."

"I'm tempted to say Mrs. Coniglio thinks she's good at all of it."

"Objection—pure conjecture," Loew bellowed.

"Sustained," said Judge Bartleby.

"Wouldn't you agree, Miss Becker, most of us would do better to skip the practitioner of the healing arts—as some in this court describe Mrs. Coniglio—and go straight to a doctor? That Mrs. Coniglio—purposely or not—tries to replace a medical doctor for cases where doctors are the only real path to recovery?"

"Maybe," said Ann.

"No further questions," said Moffat. Ann stepped down from the witness stand.

Perhaps believing, as Judge Bartleby seemed to, that the lawyers' questioning and the witness testimony were going nowhere, the people seated in the courtroom began to talk among themselves. A low buzz soon spread to every corner of the room. Banging his gavel, the Judge called the two attorneys to the bench again.

"I have no intention of having a continuance on this case," he revealed, loud enough for those standing near the bench to hear. "What I'm telling you, gentlemen, is I want a verdict by the time this court closes." That gave them an hour to finish the case.

Moffat and Loew stepped away from the Judge's Bench to converse. Soon, Loew and the bailiff had their own whispered conference, and the latter turned to face the Court. To the surprise of many, he announced: "Defense calls Mrs. Maria Coniglio to the stand." *Zia* Maria came to her feet with eagerness, all but brushing away Mr. Loew's arm as he kindly attempted to help her to the Witness Stand.

"We know you treated Nicholas Carpaccio for an illness on March 12," Loew said, when she was seated. "What made you think you could treat Mr. Carpaccio if you are not a doctor?"

"Mr. Carpaccio," the interpreter repeated her response to the lawyer's question, "had the kind of fever I can treat. Although I am not a doctor, I have knowledge of medicine, as many do. The knowledge one gets from curing many people over many years."

"I see." said Mr. Loew. "have you ever claimed to be a doctor to the people you help?"

"No," said Mrs. Coniglio.

"Your witness," said Loew.

Perhaps to intimidate her, Moffatt locked eyes with *Zia* Maria for a long time before he started to cross-examine her. He would later say there was no lack of confidence in the way she met his stare. "Mrs. Coniglio, did you tell Dr. Lawrence on March 12 that doctors could not heal the diphtheria cases in New York?"

Loew tried to cut off the interpreter's translation: "Objection, Your Honor! Total hearsay!"

"It is not hearsay. I have the notes from Lawrence's meeting with Mrs. Coniglio on March 12. 'She wanted to know why the doctors have not been able to stop the fevers,'" Moffatt quoted from a paper he held.

"That's out of context," Loew replied.

Even as Loew tried to defend his client, the interpreter provided *Zia* Maria's quick reply: "It's true the doctors cannot heal the diphtheria cases in the city."

Just what he wanted to hear, Moffatt came in for the kill: "Did you tell Dr. Lawrence his help wasn't needed, Mrs. Coniglio? That you had the epidemic under control? That the doctor's inoculations were killing people??"

Loew demanded another conference. Moffatt followed him to the bench reluctantly.

"You can see my client doesn't know she's incriminating herself…" began Loew.

"By telling the truth?" Moffatt asked.

"By allowing you to provoke and twist and tangle her words beyond comprehension. I was mistaken to put Mrs. Coniglio on the witness stand. Please, your Honor, allow her to vacate."

"This is highly irregular, Mr. Loew," said Bartleby, disapprovingly. "It's your job to counsel your client so she doesn't incriminate herself." He continued to browbeat Loew in this manner for several minutes. Finally, giving his consent for *Zia* Maria to vacate the stand, he asked Loew—just on the heels of this tongue-lashing—who his next witness would be.

"I want Lawrence on the stand," came the testy reply.

"Where did you hear about Mrs. Coniglio's famous healing powers?" was Loew's first question for Lawrence.

"Nobody said her healing powers were famous..." Lawrence said.

"Quite so. But how did you hear about them, Dr. Lawrence?" said Bartleby.

"I've already answered the question. I said from hearsay."

"What kind of hearsay?" asked Loew.

"Hearsay. That's all." Pursing his lips, Lawrence looked downward.

"Was it someone at the Board of Health, one of the police commissioners, a reporter?" Loew quizzed him.

"Maybe it was a reporter, something in the newspapers, an editorial that got you thinking about the old lady? About her miraculous healing powers. About the fact that you, with your many years of training, couldn't do as well as this poor, solitary, uneducated woman?" Loew elaborated.

Moffatt rushed in to rescue Lawrence. "I object, your Honor. This is pure conjecture."

"Sustained. Please, Mr. Loew, get to the point," the Judge said.

"That's exactly what I intend to do. With my next witness. You may step down, Dr. Lawrence. The defense calls Ann Becker."

Ann returned to the witness stand.

Mr. Loew gave her a newspaper clipping. "Can you describe what you're looking at?"

"An editorial from the New York Beacon."

"Ever see it before?" asked Loew.

"Yes. Shortly before we went to visit Mrs. Coniglio, Dr. Lawrence pointed it out to me." Becker's face reddened, and she looked, somewhat shamefaced, in the direction of her boss. Everything she was saying was true, yet she felt acutely that she was betraying him.

"What was Dr. Lawrence's reaction to the editorial?" Loew asked.

"He was infuriated with the reporter first, and then with the woman mentioned in the editorial, who turned out to be Mrs. Coniglio, because he said she was planting false security in the minds of people she came in contact with, making them believe they were safe from infectious diseases."

"And what was your answer?" asked Mr. Loew.

"I told him nobody even knew who she was. She couldn't have the sway he thought she had."

"And his response?"

Ann looked thoughtful. "He said that a woman like her could have made the Spanish Influenza much worse. That somebody had to stop her from practicing…well, doing whatever she was doing that made people come to her. That otherwise we could have a health catastrophe."

"Do you think this response was warranted?" asked Loew.

"Objection…" This came from Moffatt, but the Judge said to let the question stand.

Ann paused for a moment. Finally, looking straight ahead and talking fast: "I thought he was over-reacting. He showed me the case numbers and they were very low for Mrs. Coniglio's area of influence. I don't think he liked that she could limit diphtheria cases without his involvement."

"You think it was a blow to his ego?" asked Mr. Loew.

"Yes, I do."

"That's all, Miss Becker," said Loew.

Moffatt swept in as Ann began to descend from the witness stand. "Miss Becker…is it true Dr. Lawrence turned you down for a promotion?"

"I was never up for promotion."

Judge Bartleby's gavel interrupted. "We have news to share about this case," he announced. "Will Mr. Loew and Mr. Moffatt and the defendant approach the bench?" He motioned for Angela and the translator to join them, as well. Once everyone he summoned were at the dais, the Judge began.

"I don't mind saying this case caught my attention from the start. The defendant, an elderly woman whose life has been devoted to nurturing others. The plaintiff, the Board of Health, in the form of Dr. John Lawrence, Director of Disease Prevention. A person who has a Harvard degree, years of medical training, and a following at the Board. It puzzled me that this accomplished man went after Mrs. Coniglio, whose treatments may amount to little more than concentrated mothering. Why was Lawrence—and I'm told it was him—going after her with such zeal? Miss Becker's testimony filled in the blanks on that account.

"I have a message from Health Commissioner Copeland. He agrees to withdraw charges if Mrs. Coniglio will no longer practice her healing arts on anyone except her family. He further states she must resist sharing her opinions about city health initiatives with anyone except her family."

Loew stepped in quickly to accept, while Lawrence raised his head in a clear expression of triumph.

"Court is adjourned." When the Judge pounded his gavel one last time for the day, *Zia* Maria walked slowly back to the defense table—quite alone as the others spoke among themselves. While she drew on her coat to leave, Dr. Lawrence approached Judge Bartleby, saying he needed to talk to him about some other matters.

"Now you remember what the Judge said, Mama?"

Zia Maria threw her arms up in the air with impatience. Her fine court clothes no longer adorned her, and she was in her old, worn housecoat, slippers on her feet, her hair unwashed and untidy. It was 3:00 o'clock in the afternoon. She had just risen from her bed.

"He remanded you into my custody and I have to make sure you follow his conditions. That means you can't wrap wool around anybody's legs or arms anymore. You can't make chicken soup for the sick, or cast spells, or set broken bones. That's all over."

Zia Maria looked away forlornly while her daughter spoke. She had always loved Angela, her youngest, from the very depths of her soul. But lately she was getting bored and disillusioned with her daughter, who was taking the court order too seriously.

"Okay, okay," she agreed. "But how am I going to spend my time? There's nothing to do now. I can't talk to my clients anymore, because they all want me to do things for them. How am I going to tell them I can't?"

"Go out and meet Lina on the playground. She loves when you spend time with her."

Zia Maria received with indifference the farewell kiss her daughter gave to her before departing.

Following Angela's advice mainly to keep on her good side, *Zia* Maria pulled on her coat and trudged to the children's playground. How, she wondered, could her daughter make her do what the Judge wanted with such vigor? Ahhh—America— where the children run wild and then side with strangers against their parents!

Yet…all was not lost. Reaching inside her pocket she pulled out a Saint's picture and some licorice. Lina would be thrilled by the image of Santa Lucia, patroness of the eyes. And of course, she loved licorice, which *Zia* Maria was always certain to buy from the penny candy store when she was shopping on Mulberry Street.

Approaching where the child sat in her customary place on the curb, *Zia* Maria was astounded to see Lina in the company of her mother that day. The women exchanged some words in dialect, and *Zia* Maria proffered the licorice and Saint's picture to the delight of the little girl.

This was the moment that *Zia* Maria caught sight of Ann Becker. How out of place she looked in that neighborhood of obscure housewives and humble laborers, her pressed suit trumpeting her own brand of foreignness as she ambled the sidewalk. At more or less the same time a black car zipped into a vacant spot along the curb.

After attempts by both women to talk to each other, Lina's mother took up the role of translator for *Zia* Maria and Miss Becker.

"Miss Becker is happy to see you, *Zia* Maria," said Lina's mother, as the old woman nodded. "She wants to tell you she is leaving New York. But she will never forget you."

With this, Ann took *Zia* Maria's hand and pumped it. *Zia* Maria put her arms around Ann to kiss her cheek warmly. Then Ann captured Lina's hand gently and walked with her to the automobile.

"She'll be back," Ann said to *Zia* Maria reassuringly. And they were gone—speeding off in that impossibly big car.

"*Terribili*," *Zia* Maria ruminated. The only reason left for her to get out of bed was gone. She and Lina's mother walked to a worn wooden bench near the playground and sat down. Why, oh why, would the Board of Health make away with a perfectly healthy youngster like that? *Zia* Maria asked. It was the birthmark, came the reply. Dr. Lawrence had an order from the Judge.

Ahhh...of course. And the two women nodded briefly. Soon their eyes had wandered away from each other, to rest instead on the buildings surrounding them, the strip of road running before the bench where they sat.

The Board of Health was thorough, Zia Maria told herself. First, they took her work, and now they had gotten her best friend.

Oooffa, how her limbs were aching. She should go back to make an ointment or plaster to chase away these infernal pains. But now the church bells were ringing and made her think, as they always did, about how much she would like to be with Rosario again. Surely, her life had merited eternity together in Paradise for them?

"You know," said Lina's mother before taking her leave of *Zia* Maria, "it's only because the doctor came here to see you that he found out about Lina. Her life will be different without the birthmark. She will be happy."

When she left, *Zia* Maria spent a long time thinking about what the other woman had said.

God's ways were indeed a mystery, but it would seem He had answered one of her prayers at last. For if the only reason Dr. Lawrence knew of Lina's mole was because he came to talk to *Zia* Maria about her healing powers, she had played an important role in the Almighty's plan for the little girl. Knowing this, *Zia* Maria could not help but feel proud and satisfied that she had been an instrument in the Lord's work.

Of course (and now she chastened herself, gently) she should have taken it all on faith from the beginning. Faith that Lina had been taken away for the best. Faith that being deprived of her healing practice was for the best. Faith that God was watching her and Lina and her clients, even the bootleggers like Nick and Johnny Carpaccio in jail—knowing and blessing and keeping them in his hands. All of them. All for the best.

She sighed heavily. She would go to church now and talk to the Lord. Perhaps together they could find a way for her to help her neighbors again.

And *Zia* Maria rose to her feet slowly, stretching first one calf, then the other. "The disease which plagues you will kill you," she reminded herself ruefully. Then she began to walk, with timid deliberation and a sense of mission, toward the bells.

AUTHOR'S NOTES

My book is based on my father's stories about growing up in Little Italy, Manhattan, and tales about the experiences of his relatives back in Sicily before he was born. That is, there is some part of his telling of a story in each of the six stories composing Little Italy Diary. Some stories contain a good amount of the detail he was inclined to put into his recollections, others are more character-driven, very often centered around a person or type of person he told us about.

Therefore, there's a good deal of my own fabrication in most of the stories, but all of it reflects the solid research I've conducted over the years to ensure as much authenticity as I could as regards characters, places, attitudes, customs, speech, and history as they relate to a given tale.

If I were to include a bibliography, it would include the eminent works I have read for my research, including The Way the Other Half Lives (Jacob Riis); Milocca: A Sicilian Village (Charlotte Gower Chapman); A History of Public Health (George Rosen); Italian Folktales (Italo Calvino); Sicilian Folk Medicine (Giuseppe Pitre); Italy, From Revolution to Republic (Spencer M.

DiScala); The Leopard, (Giuseppe Di Lampeusa), and many more titles. But even as I strived for realism and authenticity, I never lost sight of the fact that the major objective of my book was to entertain. I leave it to my readers to tell me if I reached that objective.

I have mentioned the elements of my father's stories that influenced or were included in each of the stories in my book, below:

Harry Cohan – There was a cop named Harry Cohan who walked the beat in the area of lower Manhattan where my Dad grew up. My father was sort of a study geek, but had 3 older brothers to protect him, so the punishment taken by Leo, his counterpart in the story, was not my father's experience. He had one brother who was said to know the "wise guys". Dad's geekiness and the one brother's street smarts gave me two archetypes as the co-narrative for the parts of the story that really happened.

What happened "in real life" is this: Harry Cohan caught my father, his brother, and other kids making a fire on the asphalt in the street, which was a big no-no. He chased the kids, who gave him a run for his money through the maze of streets, up and down fire escapes, across a few rooftops, and finally to the apartment where my Dad's family lived. The policeman, who was outside the building said: "You have to come down sooner or later." My uncle responded with a Bronx cheer and the words: "You're full of shit, we live here!"

That is the kernel of the story that I turned into what is basically a coming-of-age tale centered around sibling rivalry. Anything other than the above is my invention.

Rosalia's Revenge – My grandmother came to New York when she was 16 years old. After coming to New York, she at some point ran into one of the local nobility from where she lived in Sicily. My grandmother tried to curtsey to the woman, who instantly rebuffed her: "We don't do that in this country, Angelina". Anything in the story outside of this foundational incident is my own invention.

Vita – There are really only a couple of facts coming from my father in this story. My grandmother had to cross the ocean alone (a big deal for a young girl from a small village) because her sister who was supposed to accompany her was diagnosed with trachoma-an eye disease-before she could make the crossing herself.

The rest of the story is my creation, allowing me to explore the problematic relationship between Northern and Southern Italians, the various reasons that people immigrated, and the constraints on women and young people at that time and place.

Paolo Visits the Baron – Much of this story is largely intact in terms of my father's telling. It runs off the earlier incident in the Introduction about my great-grandfather who died from a broken arm that got infected while he was bringing in the baron's grapes. At the age of 14 my grandfather, now head of a family in dire circumstances, went with his grandfather to see the local baron to ask for help.

Upon meeting the baron, my grandfather refused to take off his hat, as was the custom for peasants to do in the presence of the nobility. He was vocal in saying he would not do it because Italy was united, and the peasants and nobility were now equal. The baron agreed with him, and presumably helped where he could, although my grandfather did end up immigrating to the U.S. a few years later. It is absolutely true my grandfather did not know what a rug or coffee was, much to the baron's astonishment.

The Hat – This story portrays a deep concern with class consciousness and the importance of keeping to one's place in the Sicilian mindset of the time. The woman in the story is the selfsame Vita who came to America to avoid the consequences of having had premarital sex. Once in America, she finds she must get married, which is basically the reason for being, not only for women, but for every Sicilian person at the time. She finds her efforts to get a husband impeded not only by rumors that she had a boyfriend, but also by her stubborn insistence on wearing a hat that is considered a pretense for her social class. Notably, her fiancé (whose heroic qualities are based on the family's regard for my grandfather) has the lauded virtue of knowing his place. It is this innate humility and the compassion that he shows for his future wife that is the foundation for the love that is universally bestowed on Orlando, the story's hero.

The attitudes toward premarital sex, class, women and the place of family in relation to marriage are important themes in the story. All the proverbs, including the "dueling proverbs" in the scene between Orlando and Benedetto, are genuine.

Only the earlier mentioned fact that my grandmother crossed the ocean alone after her sister was restricted from immigrating is directly tied to a story from my father.

The Witch on Bleecker Street - My father astounded his four kids by talking about individuals who lived in his building whom he referred to as "witches" or "bootleggers". His family lived next to a particular women who claimed to be a witch and who was probably familiar with some of the spells, healing remedies, and magic potions from Pitre's book, Sicilian Folk Medicine. It is from this book that I found most of the folk medicine Zia Maria uses in the story.

My father also rubbed shoulders with bootleggers. The exact attitude he and his family and neighbors had towards these individuals I don't know. Usually when he spoke about bootleggers it was more or less as an aside "he was a bootlegger" to explain some quirk or action by the individual in question.

I spun my own story around my father's references to witches and bootleggers and found a way to work in little Lina, a five-year-old with a mole that caused her to be bullied. Her character is based on a true story about my aunt, who had a growth on her face that caused a doctor to take her away from her family to have the growth removed. She was returned, and as far as I know, everything turned out fine.

Some family members have told me this didn't happen, and I wrestled with that question for years, until I started researching my book and learned there were absolutely cases where American health authorities temporarily removed people to a health facility—children in particular—who had illnesses or conditions they thought were not treated adequately by their "foreign" parents.

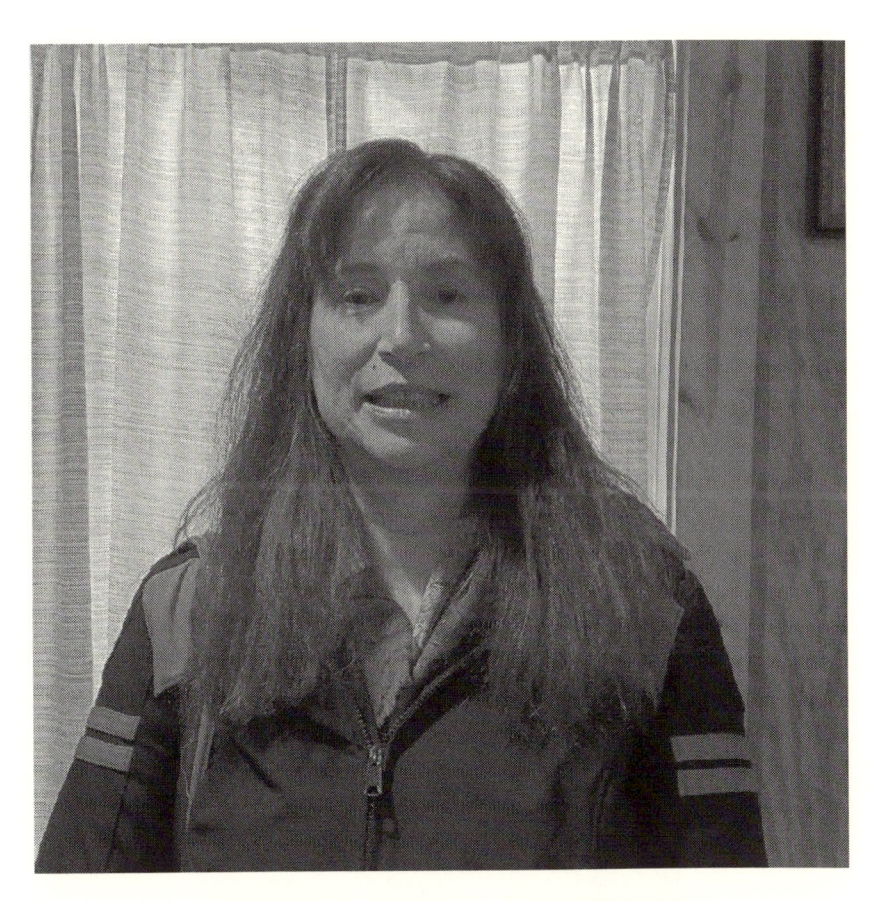

ABOUT THE AUTHOR

Angela Edwards is a poet and short story writer presently living in Southern Maryland. "Little Italy Diary" is her first published book. Her poetry has been printed in literary magazines including "The Journal of New Jersey Poets," "Tribeca Poetry Review," and "The Potomac Review." She makes her living as a technical writer.

Follow the author in Goodreads:

https://www.goodreads.com/author/show/19858179.Angela_Edwards

Email the author at:

BleeckerStreet1000@gmail.com

Family Photos

My mother and father-to whom my book is dedicated- posing for a photo on the day of their marriage, in 1960.

A picture of my grandmother and her brother taken circa 1905. Immigrants dressed in their best clothes to pose in pictures to be sent to their families in Italy. In this frame, my grandmother is about the same age as the protagonist in the story "Vita".

This is my father with my grandfather, outside of the Brooklyn brownstone where they lived in the 1940s and 1950s, after the family moved out of lower Manhattan. Immigrants left the early Italian enclaves when their lives became more economically stable.

A photography studio shot of my ten-year-old father, taken about 1923 for the occasion of his confirmation into the Roman Catholic faith. This is the age of Leo in the story "Harry Cohan".